Marcus Lehmann

ITHAMAR

Translated from the German

FELDHEIM PUBLISHERS Ltd.
Jerusalem New York

Originally published in German
under the title Itamar

First published in English, 1981
ISBN 0-87306-282-5

Phototypeset at the Feldheim Press

Philipp Feldheim Inc.
96 East Broadway
New York, NY 10002

Feldheim Publishers Ltd
POB 6525 / Jerusalem, Israel

Printed in Israel

I

ELYAKIM BEN CHIZKIYAH

I REJOICED WHEN THEY SAID to me, 'Let us go up to the House of the Lord!' Our feet were standing within your gates, Jerusalem; Jerusalem built as a compact city, where the tribes went up, the tribes of the Lord, as a testimony to Israel, to give thanks to the Name of the Lord. For there were set thrones for judgment, the thrones of the house of David. Pray for the peace of Jerusalem, may they prosper that love thee. Peace be within your walls and prosperity within your palaces. For the sake of my brethren and my companions I will plead for peace within you. For the sake of the House of the Lord our God, I will request your good." (Psalm 122)

Thus sang the Psalmist when he greeted the sublime city, the city of the great King. But now,* this glory has disappeared, and rubble and ruins present a depressing picture to the visitor. In spite of this, Jerusalem is still a city of a peculiar and mysterious charm. The view from

*In the late nineteenth century.

the Mount of Olives over the city is strangely beautiful and extraordinarily attractive and stimulating, leaving an indelible impression upon the mind. Nobody who has attained the merit of enjoying this sight can ever forget it. In the north, crowned with a minaret, gleams the height of Nebi Samuel, perhaps the site of the Biblical Mizpah, from which many a weary pilgrim caught his first glimpse of Zion. In the east we see only gray, bare, cleaved, rugged hills, descending steeply into the Jordan valley to the mysterious salt sea, which we call the Dead Sea, constituting the lowest depression on earth (394 meters below sea level). Here the air is so pure and transparent that we can imagine ourselves already touching and holding the quiet water in our hands. Nevertheless, the Dead Sea is still many miles away, and its surface is no less than 1189 meters below the peak of the mountain on which we are standing! On the opposite bank of the Jordan and the Dead Sea there rises a long mountain range, broken intermittently by wild gorges, which form the bed of the waters of the Arnon and of other mountain streams. The Arnon flows from the mountains of Gilead in the north to the mountains of Moab in the south. When evening approaches and the sun is low, and the white heights in the foreground of the landscape have lost their brilliance, the coloring of the distant mountains is infinitely beautiful. The changing light brings out such a wealth of varying shades of color, that it would be impossible to reproduce them on canvas. The view to the west, which can be enjoyed to best advantage in the early hours of the morning, comprises the entire city of Jerusalem. Every hill, every valley, even every outstanding building, can be clearly recognized, and it is easy to get an accurate picture of the positions of all the various parts of the city in relation to one another. If you look down upon the city from this favorable vantage point on the Mount of Olives, you will be surprised at first by the ragged and dilapidated appearance of certain areas of Jerusalem, and you will gaze with repugnance at the amount of rubbish which has accumulated in and around the city. The old, deep gulley of Tyropacon which bisected the center of the area is now only a flat depression in the ground. The wild gorge, which contained the lake of Bethesda, is now entirely covered up. Heaps of rubble are embedded in the Kidron valley. The rocky hills, once climbed by Yo'av, have been turned into hillsides where corn and vegetables grow. The extensive cemeteries surrounding Jerusalem on almost all sides, make a very sad impression on the viewer, which is increased by the deep silence brooding over the city most of the day and the dull gray color of the domed houses. Indeed, Jerusalem has changed greatly since the time when the Psalmist could sing affectionately, "Delightful height, joy of all the land!"

The ground descends to the dry bed of the Kidron, and then rises again suddenly to the top of Mount Moriah, where the holy area of Haram al-Sherif is now located. This most awe-inspiring site is planted with cypresses and olive trees and surrounded by walls of such exalted beauty that even in decay they subject the mind to an overpowering emotion, more than any other building on earth. On the southern part of the Haram stands the Mosque of El Aksa and a group of buildings which once provided accommodation for Temple pilgrims. Almost in the center of the strange site we are viewing rises a platform paved with stones, whose center in its turn bears the famous Dome of the Rock. Within the confines of this sacred area stood the Temple in ancient times.

But it was altogether different at the time of our story. On the Temple Mount stood the holy House of God, which had been enlarged and rebuilt in glorious splendor by King Herod, and the great men of Judea lived in magnificent palaces. One of the most noble and worthy citizens of Jerusalem was Elyakim, son of Chizkiyahu. His palatial home was situated on the road leading to the Water Gate. Besides this house, he possessed many fields and vineyards, which were tilled by numerous slaves, while other slaves tended his flocks, consisting of thousands of sheep, goats and cattle. Great elegance was displayed in the house, which contained chests filled with golden and silver vessels. Elyakim was a descendant of one of the noblest families of Judah. Nachshon ben Aminadav, the first prince of Judah, was among his ancestors. But Elyakim was distinguished not only for his wealth and noble descent. He was generally respected for his piety, his virtuous way of life, his charity to the poor, and above all, for his great learning. As a youth he had sat at the feet of Hillel the Wise and had been acknowledged by him as one of his most outstanding pupils. Unlike the majority of the noble and wealthy citizens of Jerusalem, Elyakim had not joined the pleasure-loving Sadducees, but had remained a faithful adherent of the unaltered and complete faith of Israel. Elyakim had suffered much unhappiness. The beloved wife of his youth had borne him twelve children, sons and daughters. Eleven of them had died in early childhood, and at the birth of the twelfth child, the mother had closed her eyes forever. Deep mourning for the loss of his precious wife did not prevent Elyakim from educating his only son, Ithamar, with the greatest care. He guarded him like the apple of his eye. He was the light of his eyes, the delight of his heart.

II

SEEDS OF HATE

THE HOLY TEMPLE WAS STILL standing, and all the institutions of the Jewish people were flourishing. Sacrifices were offered up every day, as prescribed in the Torah. Three times a year, the tribes went up to Jerusalem, in order to appear before the Holy Presence of God. The *Sanhedrin* had its seat in the square hall of the Holy Temple, from where it dispensed justice. Many great men and pious scholars instructed the people concerning the path they ought to follow. In spite of this, the nation was already approaching disintegration with inexorable steps. Political and religious disagreements divided the people and changed men who ought to have loved each other as brothers into mortal enemies. In the sphere of religion a bitter struggle was taking place between two camps—the Pharisees and the Sadducees. The wealthy and the nobility generally belonged to the latter sect. They denied the validity of the Oral Law and did not believe in the immortality of the soul. Their main aim was the fullest possible enjoyment of life upon earth. They were opposed by the Pharisees (i.e. *Perushim*, or

Separatists). These were pious and holy men who had made the study of the law of God the chief purpose of their life. The majority of the people followed the Pharisees, so that the Sadducees could never have a permanent influence on the organization of Jewish institutions, though the sympathies of their kings were frequently with them. Conflict between political rivals was equally fierce. The antagonism between the two Hasmonean princes, Hyrcanus and Aristobulus, resulted in the decline of that heroic family, and Herod, an Idumean slave favored by the Romans, usurped the throne of Judea. The last king of the Hasmonean dynasty was led into captivity by the Romans, while Herod forced Mariamne, the last remaining descendant of that famous house, to become his wife. As you can well imagine, the Jewish people did not love this ruler who had been forced on them. He had established his throne upon corpses and ruins and could only maintain it with the aid of the Romans. He ordered the members of the Great Assembly to be slain, since they represented the Law which prohibits a foreigner who is also a slave from ascending the Jewish throne. Only one member of the Great Assembly was left alive by Herod's decree, and he was blinded. Later Herod repented sincerely of his cruel deeds and attempted to win the love of the people by enlarging the Holy Temple and re-establishing it in splendid glory. But love cannot be bought, and though he did acquire the affection and to some extent the admiration of the Romans, the people of Judea still despised the usurper who had burdened his soul with innumerable crimes. Throughout Herod's reign there were repeated disturbances and rebellions followed by bloody punishment and persecutions. Hillel and Shammai, the two heads of the re-established *Sanhedrin*, kept aloof from all party politics and sought only to maintain the greatest treasure of the nation, the holy law of God, and to encourage the study of the Law. Most of their pupils followed their example, and Elyakim too kept aloof from the political turmoil, endangering neither his life nor his property.

When Herod died, one of his sons, Archelaus, succeeded him under the title of Ethnarch (prince of the people). He was no better than his father. Since he did not know how to keep the favor of the Romans he was deposed and banished to Gaul. Now Judea became a Roman province, to the deep sorrow of all Jewish patriots.

At this time, Ithamar, the only son of Elyakim, had grown into a handsome youth of eighteen. Elyakim wished his son and heir to marry the beautiful Tirtzah, the daughter of his friend Elazar, who was also the descendant of a noble and wealthy family. Elazar too favored this match, and there seemed to be no obstacle to the marriage of the young couple. There was only one individual whose mind was filled with rage at the thought that Ithamar was to be the husband of the beautiful Tirtzah. This man was a lowly slave named Orev, born in Elyakim's house. For many generations the ancestors of Orev had been in bondage to Elyakim's family. All of them had served their masters faithfully and were regarded as part of the family, as was the custom among Jews. Orev was considered as being his master's right hand. He was in charge of the household, the steward set over the farms, and the shepherds and their flocks were under his personal supervision. He was also responsible for the accounts, with both income and expenditure passing through his hands. When his master had raised him to this high position, he served him with increased fidelity and care, hoping to receive his freedom as a reward for his services. Orev was thirty years old. He had refused to marry a slave girl and was forbidden to marry a free Jewess. Once, when his master had advised him to choose a wife for himself, he had replied, "My master, I have served you faithfully for as long as I can remember. You have made me administrator of your property and steward of your household, and your possessions have always increased in my hands. I have never asked you for a special reward. But today, when you advise me to choose a wife, I beg you to give me my freedom so that I may set up a house of my own and need not take a slave for a wife. I will remain in your service for whatever wage you care to give me, and I shall look after your property in faith and sincerity."

"My dear Orev," Elyakim replied, "your speech makes me sad. You know how much I love you and how much I respect your diligence and your skill, your faithfulness and reliability. I would gladly give you your freedom, but a divine prohibition forbids it. The Torah says concerning bond slaves, 'You shall pass them on to your children after you as inherited property, they shall serve you forever.' It follows from this that we are not allowed to grant the bond slave his freedom. I know very well that there are teachers in Israel who teach that the above verse does not contain any prohibition, but merely permission to keep the slaves in bondage forever, so that there is no religious obstacle to granting them freedom. Still, my teacher Hillel, of blessed memory, held the former view, and I follow his view in everything. Therefore, I regret that I am unfortunately unable to fulfill your wish. Ask for something else, my Orev, as reward for your faithful service, and I will gladly grant it, if it is within my power to do so."

Orev was silent. He knew that any further effort in this direction was useless. But his mind was filled with rage, and thoughts of vengeance arose in him.

However, he hid his anger in his heart while remaining as friendly and obedient to his master and his son as before.

A little later, when Tirtzah, the daughter of Elazar, had blossomed into a charming young girl, it was decided to choose her as a wife for Ithamar. When Orev heard of this, his passion flared up. He swore a holy oath to win Tirtzah for himself and destroy Ithamar. Thus he planned to avenge himself on the most tender feelings of his master, whose only son was his most precious possession on earth.

III

A BANISHED HIGH PRIEST

SINCE THE HASMONEAN princes no longer occupied the office of the high priest, the kings, and later on the Romans, bestowed this high office on their personal favorites. Usually bribery was the decisive factor in the appointment. He who was able to offer the greatest bribe to the Roman procurator through his relations or friends, received the honor of the high priesthood. Therefore, this holy office was usually occupied by unworthy men, many of whom kept their position for less than a year. The high priest alone was permitted to enter into the Holy of Holies and this only once a year, on the Day of Atonement. If an unworthy man entered this holy place and did not perform the sacrifice as the Law demands, death struck him down on the holy site. After the elders of the *Sanhedrin* had prepared the high priest to perform the holy service on the Day of Atonement, they implored him, in the Name of Him who had chosen to dwell in the Holy Temple in Jerusalem, to proceed exactly according to the Law. Tears filled the eyes of the sages when they had to speak in this manner, and the high priest, with an uneasy presentiment, departed from them crying. On the Day of Atonement, when the time drew near for the high priest to enter the Holy of Holies, the hundreds and thousands gathered in the forecourts and on the Temple Mount waited anxiously in breathless suspense for the moment when the high priest should return. If he emerged in peace, every heart was filled with great joy. But if he did not emerge, his corpse was pulled out from the Holy of Holies on a chain. Then the fast day became a day of mourning for Judea.

At the time of our story, Valerius Gratius had been appointed as administrator of the land and as procurator. He deposed High Priest Anan and entrusted Ishmael, the son of Phiabi, with this high office. Ishmael was one of the most worthy high priests. Our sages tell us that when he took up his new appointment, a heavenly voice called out: "Lift up your heads, O Gates, so that Ishmael ben Phiabi may enter, a worthy successor to High Priest Pinchas!"

He had to perform the unusual task of preparing the ashes of the red cow (*parah adumah*). Spring water, with a pinch of this ash added to it, was sprinkled on the impure on the third and seventh day of their impurity. The first ash for purification had been prepared by Elazar, the son of the High Priest Aharon, under the guidance of Moses. Only seven instances of the preparation of such ash were recorded in the course of 1300 years, and the preparation of the seventh was the task of High Priest Ishmael ben Phiabi. The most meticulous care was taken to perform the preparation in purity. Seven days prior to the burning of the cow, the high priest had to leave his home and move to a hall in the Holy Temple called the House of Stone. There, he was sprinkled daily with the remaining water of purification. Then the high priest and his followers moved to the Mount of Anointment, where the elders of the *Sanhedrin* were already awaiting him. There was a bathhouse there where the priest had to immerse himself again. Then the cow was bound and placed upon a pile of wood. The priest slaughtered it, collected the blood and sprinkled it seven times while facing the Holy of Holies. For each sprinkling, he had to immerse his finger again in the blood, and when the sprinkling was completed, he set the pile of wood alight. As soon as the flames attacked the body of the cow and it burst open, the priest took hold of a log of cedar wood and showed it to the assembled people three times, asking each time, "Is this log of cedar wood?" The assembled people responded, "Yes." He proceeded in the same way with the hyssop and the crimson thread. Then he rolled them all together and threw them into the fire of the burning cow. Finally, the ashes were collected and divided into three parts. One third was deposited in an outer building adjoining the forecourt of the Holy Temple. One third was preserved on the Mount of Anointment, and one third was distributed to the twenty-four divisions of the priestly families.

It was the privilege of the greatest and most saintly men of Israel, such as Moshe, Ezra, Shimon the Just and Yochanan the High Priest, to conduct the burning of the *parah adumah*. Ishmael ben Phiabi now joined the ranks of these great men. As you can imagine, the affection and admiration of the people for this worthy and holy priest increased greatly as a result. But this great admiration itself led to his downfall. The envious Romans could not bear that one man should enjoy such widespread popularity and admiration. Thus, Valerius Gratius ordered High Priest Ishmael to be deposed and bestowed this supreme office upon another, Elazar ben Anan, of the family of Sheth. Every Jewish heart was then filled with great sadness. They had been so happy to possess such a worthy, God-fearing high priest, and now the Romans interfered in the most sacred rights of the nation with brutal force, deeply wounding their pride. Of course, Valerius Gratius attempted to justify his actions. The circle surrounding the high priest had caused various complaints to be raised. His sons and sons-in-law had occupied the most influential positions, and their slaves had committed many cruel acts (*Pesachim* 57a). The only complaint which could be laid against the deposed high priest himself was that he had not been firm enough in supervising those close to him. But the people did not consider this sufficient reason for removing this highly esteemed man from the dignity of the high priesthood. Though the Romans had been hated previously for their brutality, greed and the cruel manner in which they collected impossibly high taxes and duties, this hatred now increased greatly and reached its highest peak. Hot-blooded youths made no secret of their feelings and expressed their anger at every opportunity. As a result, many youths were called to account for their deeds and punished most severely. Consequently, all took care not to express in public what they felt in their hearts. Still the bitter feelings of the people grew in strength.

Ithamar, the son of Elyakim, was also filled with anger against the acts of violence perpetrated by the Roman administrator and his cohorts. But his father warned him every day to keep away from the activities of all political parties.

"Fear God and the king, my son, and do not mix with those who want to change the existing order of things. God has decreed that we must serve the Romans. It is true that Edom treats us badly and shows us evil and never good. Still, that is the will of the Omnipotent, in order to punish us for our numerous sins. Therefore it is not good to rebel against the yoke of Edom. When the time for redemption arrives, God will send us the Redeemer and we shall humiliate Esav. But if we attempt to break our chains in impotent rage before the time of redemption has come, we shall only heap destruction upon our own heads. Therefore I beg of you, my son, keep away from the rebels."

IV

THE YOUNG ROMAN

WHILE ELYAKIM SPOKE THUS to his son, a messenger arrived from the palace of the procurator to invite young Ithamar to the palace. Caius Cimber, a noble young Roman and former playmate of Ithamar, had arrived there and wished to see his friend. The young Roman's father had occupied the office of tax collector in Jerusalem for many years and had been a friend of Elyakim. Five years earlier he had returned to Rome. Now his son was on his way to Caesarea in order to enroll in the Syrian army. He had come to Jerusalem especially in order to see his former playmate Ithamar. Ithamar accompanied the messenger who led him into the garden of the palace. Next to some bushes of oleander and myrtle, Caius was sitting, eagerly reading the odes of Horace inscribed on a parchment scroll. When he heard the approaching steps, he jumped up. "Ithamar, atavis regibus! Amice!" (Ithamar, descendant of ancient kings! Greetings to you, my friend!) he called out. The youths embraced.

"How tall and strong you have grown," exclaimed

Ithamar, regarding his friend. "If your messenger had not told me that you were expecting me, I would not have recognized you!"

"You too are no longer the little boy of five years ago. I would not have recognized you either had I not expected you to accept my invitation. How handsome you have grown, Ithamar!"

"So have you, Caius. And you want to be a soldier, I have heard."

"Certainly. Mars rules the world. Rome has already conquered a considerable portion of the world, but there are still enough unconquered nations. I shall march forward with our army, first to the east, following in the footsteps of Alexander of Macedonia, until we reach India where there are still many rich countries to conquer for Emperor Tiberius. My arm is strong, and I have strengthened it further by fighting in the arena. I have great courage and intend to distinguish myself in battle. The best teachers of Rome have instructed me in the science of war, so that I know how to lead men in combat and to encircle fortified cities, to break their walls and conquer them by storm. Soon I shall lead a cohort and rise from one rank to the next. I am convinced that Mars favors me. When I return to Jerusalem one day, I shall be procurator of Judea, and then you, my dear Ithamar, shall become the high priest."

Ithamar smiled. "You have ambitious plans, my Caius," he said. "I hope that they will all be fulfilled for you. As for me, I absolve you already of your promise. I can never become a high priest. I am not a descendant of

Aharon but of Nachshon, the first prince of the tribe of Judah!"

"What would you like to be?"

"I shall plant my land, as my father did before me. I shall till my vineyard, look after my flocks and occupy myself with the study of the Torah."

"Then you may become a member of the *Sanhedrin* one day!"

"That is my most ambitious aim."

The Roman regarded Ithamar with pity. "I am grateful to you, Mars," he said, "that I was born a Roman nobleman and not a Jew! How narrow is your outlook, how low the aim you have set yourself! An honorable position in Judea and that is all. Then the real enjoyment of life remains completely closed for you. You will move from the fields and flocks to the synagogue, from there to the house of study and on to the Temple, then back to grow cabbages or press olives. That will be the course of your daily life. How different will my future be! When I return to Rome victorious, I shall be exalted by the emperor, admired by the people and honored by the fathers of the city. Then there will be feasts, banquets, games, and the wine will overflow in the jugs. Dice will be cast in cups, and Venus shall be worshiped to the sound of delightful music, beneath a shower of sweet scented flowers."

"What you have just described, my dear Caius, is the life of a Roman. We Jews have different aims in life. The one and only God, the omnipotent Creator of the universe, has chosen us to be His people. More than thirteen hundred years ago the Egyptians ruled over us as the Romans do now. There followed a succession of other peoples, notably the Assyrians, the Babylonians, the Persians, the Medes and the Greeks. Their power was broken, their rule cast off, while Judah remained strong and powerful. All the peoples who have ruled the world rose temporarily upon the ladder of power, fame and esteem till they reached the summit, and then their power declined. Now they have all turned to dust. Proud Rome, too, will share their fate, though perhaps only in the more distant future. The day will surely come when the Capitol will fall in ruins and Jupiter Capitolinus and all Roman gods will fall with it. But Judah remains forever, since our God is Eternal. He keeps us upright and protects us forever. You see, my dear Caius, we live for the service of the Omnipotent God and dedicate ourselves to Him since that is our supreme ambition."

"Foolish talk! How can you compare Judea with Rome! Judea is but a speck of dust, while Rome is the whole world!"

"You may be right, my dear Caius; Rome is superior to Judah in many respects. But Judah's inhabitants are the chosen people of the Omnipotent God. Who is the greatest man in Rome? The emperor. After him the greatest man is he whom the emperor favors with his love, and after that a person's greatness still depends on his proximity to the emperor. But who is the emperor compared to the only God, the Master and Creator of the universe? The omnipotent God has chosen us to be His people. He has given us our laws, fought our battles and won our victories. He loves us even when He punishes us for our sins. He chastises us in order to lead us back to the right path and to keep us alive. The highest achievement of man is proximity to God. Man can only approach Him through a virtuous life, obedience and love for Him. This leads us to a sublime state of bliss which cannot be compared with the dissolute joys you have described to me before."

"But why have you not been more successful? Why are you a defeated and subservient nation?"

Ithamar paled with anger and clenched his fists. Caius noticed that his friend was deeply hurt.

"I did not mean to offend you," he said kindly. "Let us remain friends and not part in disagreement. I must leave Jerusalem and travel to Caesarea this very day, for our legions will soon start on their triumphant march of victory. You are a Jew and I am a Roman, so our outlook on life is bound to be different. When we played together many years ago we were small children, and these differences were not yet apparent. Since then you have sat at the feet of Gamliel, while I have enjoyed the instruction of the great masters in Rome. Our ways must part, but we can continue to remain friends. Forgive me and remain my friend!"

He stretched out his right hand which Ithamar seized, saying, "I forgive you and remain your friend."

The friends embraced and Caius accompanied Ithamar to the gate of the palace. Here they shook hands once more. "May peace be with you," said Ithamar.

"May the gods protect you," responded Caius.

Ithamar returned home, but on the way the question of why Judah was a defeated and subservient nation continued to ring in his ears.

V

THE RESCUE

When Ithamar returned home, he found his father seriously ill. The good son was extremely worried, and all the thoughts which had previously occupied his mind receded to the background on account of his anxiety for his dear father. Ithamar had no close relations other than his father. He had never known his mother, and all his brothers and sisters had died before his birth. Thus his heart was bound with passionate love to the worthy sage whose life was now in danger. Day and night he watched at his bedside and allowed himself only a few hours of rest, when Orev, the manager of the household, took his place by the patient's bedside. Large donations were distributed among the poor, and all pious and holy men living in Jerusalem prayed to God for the recovery of the widely respected and pious Elyakim. God heard their prayers and the fever left the patient, but he was so weak that the doctor ordered him not to leave his bed for some time. Sorrow, pain and many long wakeful nights had left their mark on Ithamar. He looked pale and exhausted. Elyakim regarded his son thoughtfully and said:

"My dear child, what good is my recovery if I should lose you? I no longer require careful nursing, and the servants will see that I lack nothing. Now you must take care of your own health and try to recover from the strain of the last few weeks. Go out and join the company of your friends. Orev shall accompany you everywhere and take care that you come to no harm."

Orev, who was present, could not hide a malicious gloating smile on hearing the words of Elyakim. But neither the sage nor the youth noticed this. The steward suppressed his smile and said in a sincere and humble tone, "Do not worry, dear master; I shall guard our Ithamar like the apple of my eye. Come, let us get ready for a walk immediately!"

Ithamar embraced his father and said, "My dearest father, your wish is my command. I also feel the need to breathe some fresh air."

"Would it not be a good idea if we could spend some time on your estate in Jaffa?" asked Orev. "The fresh sea air and the heavenly gardens with their delightful scents will soon bring back the bloom to Ithamar's cheeks!"

"You are right, my Orev," said Elyakim. "Go together to Jaffa and stay there for a few weeks."

"But I don't like to leave you for so long, my father," replied Ithamar.

"You cannot give me any greater joy nor help me more to regain my good health than by looking after your own recovery, my son."

"Your will shall be done, my father."

"Prepare everything for your departure, Orev. Choose the slaves who will accompany you and the mules to carry you and your luggage." Next day, Ithamar and Orev, accompanied by ten slaves, left Jerusalem riding their mules.

Jaffa is the harbor nearest to Jerusalem. Its history goes back to ancient times. The town was already in existence when the Israelites entered the Holy Land. Here began the boat journey of the prophet Yonah when he fled to Tarshish (Jonah 1:3). Here also landed the Phoenician fleets when they brought the precious logs of cedar wood from the coast of Lebanon for the building of the Temple. At that time, however, Jaffa was not yet in Jewish hands, for they only conquered it later under the Maccabeans. From early times on, Jaffa was famous for its gardens, which are still extensive today. Though the surface soil is sandy, the lower layers of soil are particularly fertile, and there is water in abundance. The hedges surrounding the gardens consist of impenetrable cacti, which afford them excellent protection. Each individual garden has a walled-in well and an elevated water tank which is filled by a donkey turning a water wheel. The most important feature of Jaffa is its harbor, which is difficult and dangerous to approach by boat. A long row of hard, sharp rocks juts out from the foaming waves, parallel with the coast line, like a natural, protective wall of firm land. However, there remains a narrow channel of water between the rocks and the land ending in a wide semi-circle. But this channel is so shallow and uneven that only smaller vessels can find shelter there, and even they are occasionally shipwrecked there. Thus, larger ships must cast their anchor in the open sea, far from the coast, though even that presents danger in stormy seas. To this day, travelers and their luggage are unloaded separately and landed by smaller craft. But they can only disembark at the coastal pier during normal weather conditions. Owing to the dry south and east winds, it frequently happens that the sea level drops so low that the rocky sea bed of the channel is completely exposed in many places. Then the travelers have to be carried to the coast.

Ithamar and Orev had already spent eight uneventful days on Elyakim's estate near Jaffa. Ithamar had derived great benefit from his stay in the country and looked fresh and blooming once more. He was already contemplating his return to Jerusalem, since he longed for his father whom he had left still weak from his serious and exhausting illness. A terrible storm arose early one morning. Ithamar had just completed his morning prayers and was about to remove his *tefillin* when the storm began to rage. He stood by the window from where he could see far out to sea. The waves seemed to reach to the heavens and were dashed against the rocks by the storm, where they broke into innumerable particles and covered everything with a white foam. Orev too now stood by the window, watching the awe-inspiring spectacle.

"Woe to the ship that approaches our coastline now. ...Can you see that dot cast up and down by the waves like a ball? I fear it is a ship!" exclaimed Ithamar.

"Yes," replied Orev, "it is a ship. If my eyes do not deceive me, it is a Roman galley. Thus may all Thine enemies perish, O God."

"Do not speak in that manner, Orev! Who can rejoice at the destruction of the creatures of the good Lord? Let us hasten to the shore, where we may perhaps help to save them!"

"Every attempt at salvation is in vain. That ship is lost. It will soon be dashed against the rocks and smashed to pieces and sink. No boat can set out into the raging sea in this storm and try to save the crew. All those on board that ship are lost."

Ithamar was no longer listening to him for he had rushed away. Slowly Orev followed.

The seashore was crowded with people who anxiously observed the galley ship lifted up and plunged down into the depths by the waves. Suddenly a loud crashing sound was heard, and the screams of the dying could be distinguished above the noise of the storm and the tossing of the sea. The ship was smashed to pieces and its crew buried in the floods.

A few hours later the storm ceased and many corpses were washed ashore. Most of them were galley slaves who had rowed the ship, but besides these were also Roman seamen. Sadly, Ithamar walked about, gazing at the people whom death had struck down so suddenly. Then he noticed a Roman naval officer who did not appear to be quite cold yet. Quickly he called Orev, and both of them attempted to revive the man. They succeeded in their efforts, and the man, who had been so close to death, opened his eyes.

"Orev, order a stretcher," said Ithamar, "so that we can have the Roman carried home to our estate where we can nurse him until his strength returns."

Meanwhile, Orev had taken a bottle of wine from his pocket and held it to the Roman's lips. The fiery wine from Lebanon soon roused the man's latent vitality. He sat up and began speaking. "I thank you, Judeans, for the assistance you have given me, but I do not require you any longer. I feel strong again and shall now look for my ship and my companions."

"Your ship drifts upon the sea, smashed to pieces, and you are the only survivor! Follow me to my house where you can rest until you have completely recovered."

"Many thanks for your offer, but I no longer require any help. What is your name?"

"Ithamar, son of Elyakim."

"Well, Ithamar, if ever you come to Rome, remember that Anejus Serranus owes you a debt of gratitude."

VI

ELAZAR BEN CHANANYAH

ITHAMAR AND OREV SOON returned to Jerusalem. Elyakim, who had recovered sufficiently to leave his sickbed, received his only son, whose cheeks bloomed with good health, joyfully.

"My dear Orev, you must not resume your duties immediately, nor should Ithamar return at once to his studies. You must spend some more time enjoying yourselves here in order to recuperate fully. I would have preferred you to spend a few more weeks enjoying the benefits of the fresh sea-air of Jaffa. Your longing for me has brought you home earlier, but at least devote some of your time here to pleasure and relaxation. Ithamar is young and must not be left to his own devices; therefore, I beg of you, Orev, to accompany him everywhere. My son, go and join the young men of your own age and enjoy yourself with them. My friend Chananyah has a son your own age. Go to see him and become acquainted."

This friend, whom Elyakim had mentioned, was the famous Chananyah ben Chizkiyah ben Gorion. The Talmud recounts (Sabbath 13b) that he, together with his companions, wrote down *Megillath Ta'anith*. It was he, also, who ensured that the Book of Yechezkel was not excluded from Holy Scripture, which consists of twenty-four books: the Pentateuch, eight books of the Prophets and eleven books of Sacred Writings. Apart from these are various books of pious and sacred content which cannot be considered as direct products of prophetic visions or of divine inspiration. The first test of their authenticity was whether they agreed with the Torah, since no prophet has the right to teach anything which might conflict with the Torah. Now, the Book of Yechezkel contained some things which appeared to conflict with the Torah, and the *Sanhedrin* was therefore in favor of excluding it from the canon. Then Chananyah ben Chizkiyah ben Gorion stood up and said, "Surely the words of Yechezkel do not contradict the Law of Moses. It is due to our lack of understanding and to our superficial interpretation that we are inclined to see a contradiction here. I will immerse myself in the mysterious words of the prophet and shall not rest until I have proved as clear as the light of the sun that the Book of Yechezkel contains nothing that does not agree with the Torah."

He ordered three hundred jugs of oil to be brought to his attic room in order to be able to study as diligently by night as by day. God blessed his efforts so that he succeeded in elucidating the mysterious meaning of the prophet's words and convinced his colleagues of the truth of his interpretation. Therefore our sages teach, "Remember Chananyah ben Chizkiyah gratefully, for thanks to him, the Book of Yechezkel has been retained" (within the canon of Holy Scripture).

He was so important that when he had thus retired to the solitude of his study for many weeks, the sages of Israel could not dispense with his aid and counsel in determining the *halachah* (religious laws) and were obliged to hold frequent meetings in his attic room, instead of in their usual house of study. At that time the sages of Israel were divided between two schools, i.e. the school of Shammai and the school of Hillel. Although these two schools often disagreed in their way of interpreting the Torah and determining the *halachah*, they were joined in love, friendship and harmony regarding the religious precepts and the importance of diligent study. The pupils of Hillel were usually in the majority, and therefore the *halachah* was mostly decided according to their views. It happened one day that the school of Shammai represented a majority of those assembled in Chananyah's attic room. Eighteen *halachoth* were thus decided on that day according to the views of the pupils of Shammai.

It does not follow, however, that Chananyah belonged to the school of Shammai. On the contrary, he was probably a pupil of Hillel. Like his great teacher, he kept aloof from the political activities of the various parties and lived exclusively for the study of the Torah. His son Elazar had an entirely different nature. He, too, had been trained since early childhood to occupy himself with the Torah. But his fiery temperament made him extremely susceptible to the sufferings his people had to bear as a result of the Romans' quest for power and wealth. Elazar's mind was kindled with the idea of casting off the yoke of the Romans; he wished to stand at the head of his nation in order to fight for their freedom and independence. His trust in God knew no limits, and he was firmly convinced that Judea would succeed in driving out the Romans by force of arms and reestablish the throne of David. He was not moved by ambition. He himself was a descendant of a priestly family and therefore had no prospect or hope of mounting the throne of David. But he believed that redemption could and should be achieved by a brave rebellion against Roman rule leading to its complete overthrow. Elazar loved the Torah above all else, but he was convinced that only a free people was able to observe and fulfill it in its entirety. Did not conditions in Judea justify his view? How could the few who loved the Torah stand by silently while a pious and God-fearing high priest was deprived of his holy office on a vague pretext, in order to make room for an unworthy favorite of the Roman procurator?

Elazar had recently given proof of his love of the Torah and his trust in God. An old Torah scroll, copied from one which Ezra the Scribe had himself written, was offered for sale by the heirs of the former owner of the scroll. A wealthy Roman Jew, on a short visit to Jerusalem, wished to acquire it. Elazar, however, would not permit this precious Torah scroll to leave the country, so he bought it for ten thousand gulden. The Torah scroll was placed in an insignificant wooden ark, darkened by age. When, on the next day, Elazar wanted to read from his newly acquired treasure, it had disappeared together with its ark. His frantic search proved of no avail; nobody in the house had seen or moved the precious Torah scroll. Full of sadness and pain, Elazar went to the Holy Temple to pray to God. It was the custom that worshipers at the Holy Temple always turned to the right on entering. The following worshipers, however, would turn to the left: mourners, those who had been excommunicated, those who wished to pray for the sick and those who had lost some treasured possession. To the mourner, the priests would say, "May Almighty God, Who dwells in this House, comfort you." To the excommunicant, they would say, "May Almighty God, Who dwells in this House, guide your heart so that you may satisfy the Law and the ban be lifted from you." To him who came to pray for a sick person they would say, "May Almighty God, Who dwells in this House, have mercy on the sick and send him a speedy recovery." When Elazar came to implore God for the restoration of his great loss, the priests who were then present, said, "May Almighty God, Who dwells in this House, help you so that the lost property may be restored to you." Just as his father had once vowed not to leave his attic room until he had saved the Book of Yechezkel, so did Elazar speak now, "I shall not leave the House of God until God has answered my prayer." He repeated his prayers in the Temple till he received the news that the precious Torah scroll had been found. A servant, thinking that the ark, blackened with age, was old rubbish, had moved it to the storeroom for useless domestic tools, and there it had eventually been found. This experience strengthened Elazar's trust in God and made him rely even more confidently upon God's help in accomplishing the plans which he still nursed secretly in the innermost recesses of his heart.

VII

A NEW ACQUAINTANCE

OREV ACCOMPANIED ITHAMAR to Chananyah's house; at their request, a servant led them to Elazar, Chananyah's son. Elazar received them kindly. He embraced Ithamar, kissed him and said, "May we be friends, just as our fathers have always been friends. For some time I have longed to get acquainted with you more intimately. But you have always avoided the company of young people and were always to be found close to your father. He even accompanied you to the lectures of Gamliel, so that nobody was able to join you."

"My master Elyakim has nobody else in the world except for this only son, neither brother nor sister, nor wife, nor other children," said Orev. "Is it surprising that he is so closely attached to his only child? But his love of Ithamar is so great that he is willing to forgo the pleasure of his son's company in order to save him from the ill effects of staying constantly indoors, while illness confines Elyakim to the house.

"Thus pleasure can sometimes be derived from

suffering," Elazar responded. "Your father's poor health has given me the pleasure of your company today."

"Your speech makes me blush," answered Ithamar. "What pleasure can you derive from the visit of an insignificant youth like myself?"

"You are too modest, Ithamar. Though I know you only superficially, my admiration for you is great, for you are the son of Elyakim, one of the most noble and best men of our holy people. Besides, you are a pupil of our great teacher Gamliel, as I am. Go, Orev, and tell your master that Ithamar will spend the rest of the day with me. I myself shall bring him back to the arms of his father before nightfall." Orev took his leave.

"How can I entertain you, Ithamar?" asked Elazar.

"I beg you to show me the Torah scroll, whose acquisition for such a high price, and whose subsequent loss and recovery, have filled all Israel with admiration."

Elazar led him to an old-fashioned ark, opened it and took out the scroll. Then he unrolled it. "It is indeed priceless," he said. "Baruch, a pupil of Ezra, copied it with the greatest of care from Ezra's Torah scroll. My father and I have examined it from beginning to end, letter by letter, and found nothing to criticize. Thus the words of the wise King Solomon can be applied to it. 'You are entirely beautiful, my beloved, and there is no fault in you!' Look how beautifully the *shirath hayam* has been written, exactly as prescribed. But we must not unroll a scroll in vain. Look at the open page and ask me a question concerning its content, so that I may explain it to you if I can."

Ithamar regarded the open scroll thoughtfully for a while and then he said, "Moshe begins the hymn to victory with the words, 'I shall sing to the Lord for He is highly exalted, horse and rider did He plunge into the sea!' When the prophetess Miriam speaks to the women who follow her, she says, 'Sing to the Lord, for He is highly exalted, horse and rider did He plunge into the sea!' Why did Miriam not say, as Moshe had, 'I shall sing to the Lord'? Or why did Moshe not call to the sons of Israel, as Miriam called to the daughters, saying, 'Sing to the Lord'?"

"Your question is entirely justified, my Ithamar; let me have a little time to consider it." After a short interval he said, "Well, I hope to have found a satisfactory answer. But first, permit me to return the Torah scroll to its holy ark." He did this, and then proceeded, "When I thought about your question it occurred to me that you, Ithamar ben Elyakim ben Chizkiyah, have posed a question to me, Elazar ben Chananyah ben Chizkiyah. Both our grandfathers bore the name Chizkiyah. That reminded me of the pious king of that name, and then the answer to your question occurred to me. At the time of King Chizkiyahu, Almighty God helped His oppressed people in a most wonderful manner. Sancheriv, king of Assyria had conquered the major part of the world. He had destroyed the kingdom of Israel and led the ten tribes into captivity. Then Sancheriv approached with his powerful army, to subjugate the small kingdom of Judea. At that time, Chizkiyahu lay ill in bed, close to death, for God had sent him the following message through the mouth of the prophet Yeshayahu: 'Put your house in order, for you are about to die and will not live.' But Chizkiyahu did not despair. He turned his face to the wall and entreated God for mercy, crying bitterly. God heard his prayer and let him regain his health. The angel Gavriel defeated the Assyrian army, Sancheriv was forced to withdraw and was slain by his own sons. The Jews captured the rich camp of the Assyrians where the booty from all the conquered nations was heaped up. There followed years of happiness, wealth, peace and prosperity unequaled before or after. The pious king Chizkiyahu made sure that Judah served its God, observed His holy commandments and studied the Torah. But he did not sing a song of praise to the Lord, as Moshe, Devorah and David had done. Why not? The sages teach us that, since God had said, 'I shall save Israel for My own sake and for the sake of My servant David,' Chizkiyahu did not feel worthy enough to sing a hymn of praise to God, since the salvation had not been due to his merit. Similarly, the children of Israel in Egypt were not worthy of salvation, for they had served idols like the Egyptians. We find proof for this in the fact that they returned to the Egyptian idol-worship and fashioned a golden calf for themselves while they were encamped at the foot of Mount Sinai. But matters were entirely different as far as the women of Israel were concerned. It was because of the merit of the pious women that our fathers were redeemed from Egypt. The women of Israel, in their modesty and purity, had not only remained faithful to their husbands, who were forced to become slaves, but also kept away from idolatry. This is proved by their refusal to offer their golden jewelry for the creation of the golden calf. Aharon had said, 'Take the golden rings from the ears of your women' (Exodus, 32,2). But the men only brought their own rings and not those of the women (Exodus, 32,3). Should you imagine, my dear Ithamar, that the women refused because they did not want to be deprived of their golden trinkets, then the Torah will enlighten you on this point. When the time came to build the Tabernacle and to fashion its vessels, the women were more eager than the men to offer their golden jewelry for the service of the Lord. We can learn from this that the women had kept themselves aloof from idolatry in Egypt as well. Another point, before I answer your question. It says, 'Then Moshe sang and the children of Israel.' It ought to read, 'Then Moshe and the children of Israel sang.' But, in fact, Moshe was the actual singer. He was worthy of singing a hymn of praise to God, while the children of Israel could only join in the song with him. Therefore Moshe said, 'I will sing to the Lord for He is highly exalted, horse and rider did He plunge into the sea.' Miriam, on the other hand, invited the women to sing a hymn of praise to the Lord. 'Sing to Him,' she called to them, 'for you are worthy and deserve to sing a song of praise to the victorious Helper.' "

"I admire you, my dear Elazar; your explanation is very beautiful and apt."

"It is even more apt than your realize. You see, Ithamar, God helps His people even when they are not worthy and do not deserve help and salvation. He will send us victory, in spite of our unworthiness, for His great Name's sake. We are His people; He has chosen us for all time, and He will never abandon us. If only we would be men and try to shake off the yoke of Edom, God's omnipotence would surely lead us on to victory. Just as the angel Gavriel was sent once before in order to defeat the Assyrian army, thus will God send us His angel in order to destroy the Roman legions."

VIII

THE REBELS

FROM THAT DAY ONWARDS, Ithamar was filled with love and admiration for Elazar, for Elazar had roused in him ideas which had till then only lain dormant in his mind. He always seemed to hear again the words of his Roman friend. "Why are you a defeated and subservient nation?" Until then, he had answered this question by explaining that Israel had to suffer and repent for its sins. But now Elazar had convinced him that Israel would be led to victory in spite of its sins, if only it would dare to draw the sword against the oppressors, since God would help them for the sake of His great Name and for the sake of David, His servant. Soon Elazar had completely won over his impressionable friend to his own views. Ithamar kept his newly-found views carefully hidden from his father, both in order to save him anxiety and in order to continue his friendship with Elazar undisturbed. Orev, however, became his confidant. The crafty slave encouraged his fiery passion. He foresaw clearly that Ithamar was well on the way to self-destruction. The hot-blooded youth was likely to be killed by the Romans during the planned rebellion, or else he would be obliged to escape, never to return to Jerusalem. In any event, Orev schemed to become Elyakim's heir and the husband of the beautiful Tirtzah. He therefore pretended to be Ithamar's faithful friend who would not betray him to his father. Sometimes he would appear to dampen the burning zeal of the youth by drawing his attention to the dangers that threatened him, for he was sure that Ithamar's next meeting with Elazar would serve to dispel all previous warnings, as if they were blown away by the wind.

In the vicinity of Jerusalem, on the slope of the mountains, there stood an old ruined castle. It was claimed that Solomon had built it long ago and had resided in it during the hot summer months. The castle had been destroyed in the course of numerous battles. It had been a ruin for centuries, and its only inhabitants were owls, jackals and scorpions. Everybody kept away from this old ruin for fear of the wild beasts and poisonous reptiles and of a sudden collapse of the old walls. Besides, the site was considered by the people to harbor evil spirits, so that even highwaymen did not dare to take shelter there. Elazar and his friends, however, knew no fear. It was here that their secret meetings took place and their plans for the future took shape.

On a hot summer's day, Ithamar was allowed to participate at such a meeting for the first time. All those present were youths from the noblest families of Judea and included only those young men who were true to the faith of their fathers, the Torah. All of them had studied the Torah diligently, though without neglecting practice in the use of arms.

"My brothers, I have accepted a new member into our covenant of *kana'im* [zealots]!" Thus Elazar addressed the assembly. "Here you see before you my friend Ithamar, the son of Elyakim, who is probably well known to most of you. He is a descendant of Nachshon, the son of Aminadav, the first prince of Judah. The sages tell us that when the Jews went out of Egypt and were caught by the Egyptians at the Red Sea, Moshe commanded them to walk into the sea, but they were afraid. But Nachshon was not afraid for he was convinced of God's help, and he threw himself into the sea, into the middle of the flood waters, which stood upright on both sides of him like a wall. The whole of Israel followed his example. Our new friend and brother, Ithamar, is also filled with the spirit of his great ancestors, and like all of us here is ready to walk at the head of our people into battle and to victory."

"My friends and brothers," replied Ithamar, "my strength is but weak, and my arm is not skilled in the art of war. But in my heart there burns a holy flame for the happiness, greatness, freedom and independence of my people. I shall gladly offer all that God has given me as regards power and property to the service of Judah."

"Welcome, Ithamar," said one of the youths, Shimon ben Antigonus. "Since Elazar has accepted you in our midst, we trust you to join us in our struggle to free our nation from the yoke of Rome." Shimon embraced the new comrade and the others followed his example.

Then Elazar proceeded, "The main purpose of today's meeting is actually the introduction of our new friend Ithamar into our circle. We do not wish, however, to have undertaken the difficult journey to this place for this purpose alone, and we would like at the same time to make plans for the future. Do you think that the time has come to call the people to arms in order to drive the Romans out of the country? I believe the time is favorable. The people are in a considerable state of unrest. You know how they hate the Romans. Unreasonable taxes have been imposed on us, which are collected with great cruelty, while the Roman procurator rules ruthlessly. He has deposed the pious and saintly high priest, Ishmael ben Phiabi, and appointed an unworthy man as his successor. Each one of you has a wide circle of friends and followers who would immediately follow your call. Let us gather together, encircle the procurator and his cohorts in his castle, take over the Holy Temple, depose the newly appointed high priest and return Ishmael ben Phiabi to his office. The whole people will rejoice with us, fight with us, and be victorious with us!"

"Permit me to voice another opinion," said Yehudah ben Naftali, of the family of Aristobulus. "We are not sufficiently prepared; we must first gather more friends and adherents. Just as you, Elazar, have won our new friend Ithamar for our purpose, each one of us, too, ought to bring his friends and comrades to join our movement. There are still many noble families in Judah which have no representative in our group."

"Why do you want to rely on men and not on God?" replied Elazar. "From Him alone comes help and victory. When Gid'on went out against Midian, God said to him, 'Release your great fighting force and retain only three hundred men with you. With them I shall make you victorious over Midian,' and thus it came to pass. Not the size of the army assures victory, but the help of the Almighty, God. When Matithyahu rebelled against the Syrian tyranny, he did not first ask to know the aid on which he could rely, nor did he count the men gathered about him. His son Yehudah haMaccabi went out into battle against the great Greek armies with a few untrained, poorly equipped men. With the praise of God on their lips, they swung their swords and drove the brutal rulers from their homeland. Of course we cannot compare ourselves to those divinely inspired heroes. Still, God will help us for the sake of His great Name which has been desecrated by the Romans. How can we serve God as our heart demands, when we are constantly hindered by foreign rulers, and unworthy men are appointed to the office of the high priest? No! Almighty God will not tolerate it any longer. He will help us for the sake of His great Name."

IX

IN SEARCH OF A LEADER

"He will help us for the sake of His great Name!" cried out the youths, full of enthusiasm. Only Yehudah ben Naftali did not join in the joyful cry.

"Forgive me, my faithful friend Elazar," he said, "if I oppose your enthusiasm with my calm considerations. There is a time to be zealous for the Lord and to act as Pinchas did when corruption penetrated into Israel. When the evil deed took place before his own eyes, when Zimri ben Salu led his paramour through the camp, mocking at Moses and the sages of Israel, there was no time to consider and take counsel, and he pierced the evildoer together with his Midianite woman. God knows that I am ready to do likewise under similar circumstances. The prophet Eliyahu also acted zealously for the Lord when he slew the priests of Ba'al, and all of us would be ready to act likewise at any moment. This is why we call ourselves *kana'im*, zealots, because we consider these great men as our ideal. Whenever action is required, our zeal will not be lacking. But before we proceed to act, everything must be sufficiently prepared. We are about to undertake a great deed. We want to break the Romans' domination and drive them from our country. We trust in the help of Almighty God, but God does not want us to rush headlong into ruin. You appeal to the examples of Pinchas and Eliyahu for support, but I can quote an equally great personality in support of my view. When God had rejected Sha'ul, the first king of Israel, He commanded His prophet Shmuel, 'Go to Bethlehem and anoint one of the sons of Yishai as king over Israel.' Then Shmuel replied, 'If Sha'ul hears of this, will he not have me killed?' So God allowed Shmuel to pretend that he was going to Bethlehem only to offer up a sacrifice. How could Shmuel speak in such a way? Could not the Lord protect him from the persecution of Sha'ul? Why was the Lord not angered by Shmuel and why did He not ask him, 'Are you fainthearted that you are afraid to fulfill My commands? What can man do to you when I protect you!' But the Lord did not say this to Shmuel; He accepted his objections. We can learn from this that man should not rush headlong into ruin, in the hope that God will save him. Though we are permitted to rely on the Almighty's help in our great and holy enterprise, we must make sufficient preparations, so that we do not need to rely on miracles. Above all, we must wait for developments which will antagonize the people even more than they have been roused so far. My dear friend Elazar believes that the deposing of the pious high priest, Ishmael ben Phiabi, has embittered their minds enough. My dear Elazar, you judge the masses according to the emotions of your own noble heart. Believe me, most people do not care whether the high priest performs his duties in a worthy manner or not. They look only at the office and not at the worth of the person holding it. They do honor to High Priest Elazar, just as they did to Ishmael. If we should start the rebellion now and the people would not rise with us, we would sacrifice ourselves in vain and our holy plans would be spoiled for many years to come. No, let us wait for things to happen! The greedy Romans will lay even greater burdens on our people, and then a suitable opportunity will arise to call the people to arms."

A deep silence followed Yehudah's speech. Elazar also felt moved by Yehudah's words, and he too, remained silent. The silence was broken when Shimon ben Antigonus began to speak. "My friends, the words of our brother Yehudah have stirred up a thought in my mind. It makes me put a question before you that needs to be answered before we can decide to call the people to arms. Yehudah has mentioned the prophet Shmuel who was ordered to anoint David as king over Israel. When we take up arms and God blesses us with success so that the uncircumcised are chased away and Edom can no longer rule over Judea, who shall be our king then?"

"I am astonished at your question," replied Barak ben Gamala, one of the youths present. "Who is to be our king? Nobody else but Almighty God. Do you not know that Israel's demand for a king displeased the prophet Shmuel greatly, and that God said to him, 'They have not rejected you, but Me!' No, we do not wish to obey man but God alone, and His holy commandments. It would be sinful and approaching heresy if we were to acknowledge a master other than the King of the universe Himself who has said, 'The children of Israel shall be My servants, My servants and not the servants of men.' "

"You speak well, Barak," said Elazar. "That is how it ought to be, just as at the time of Moshe, Yehoshua and the Judges. That was indeed a glorious period for Israel. When they offered the crown to victorious Gid'on, he said, 'Not I shall be your king, but God shall be your king!' However, things have changed since then. The great hero, the royal singer, the man whom God favored, David, the son of Yishai, has received the kingdom as a gift from God for himself and for his descendants for all eternity."

"And do you wish to choose a king from the descendants of David?" asked Barak. "Perhaps you know one man among them whom you consider worthy to ascend the throne of David?"

"No, I know nobody among David's descendants whom I consider worthy of bearing the crown of Judah," replied Elazar. "However, I am firmly convinced that when we have cast off the yoke of Esav at the right time, God will send us the offspring of David, whom He has chosen to be king of Judah."

"If we want to choose a king," said Yosef ben Lapidoth, "we need not look far for the most worthy and best. Where could we find a better king than our brave friend and brother, Elazar ben Chananyah ben Chizkiyah ben Gorion? He is a hero, equal to Shimshon, pious and God-fearing like David, a zealot for the Lord like Pinchas, and his family is one of the noblest in Israel. Let us choose him at once as our king!"

"Not so," replied Elazar, "I am not an offspring of David. As you know, I am a descendant of Aharon. My place is not on the throne but at the altar."

"Were not the Hasmoneans also descendants of Aharon, yet they bore the crown of the king at the same time as the diadem of the high priest!"

"They did indeed sin in this matter, thus bringing about the destruction of their dynasty and Judah's slavery," said Elazar. "The kings of the house of David were genuinely humble and modest. They were the servants of their people rather than its rulers. I do not refer to the corrupt successors of David, like Achaz and Menashe. I mean the genuine, worthy sons of David, like Yehoshafat and Chizkiyahu. Their only desire was to serve the Lord and make their people happy. They did not demand preferential treatment and considered themselves bound by all the laws, while the haughty Hasmoneans, like Alexander Yannai, displayed their royal pride even before the supreme court of Israel. No! I neither wish to be your king, nor am I able to do so. When my people are free from the yoke of Rome I shall take pride to be nothing more than a humble citizen of the state, a member of the nation upon which the King of the universe has set His seal and to which He has joined His holy Name."

When Elazar had finished, Ithamar, overcome by his powerful speech, cried out, "How I admire you!"

X

THE CONSPIRACY EXPOSED

WHILE ITHAMAR EMBRACED his friend Elazar with tears in his eyes, a boy came running in and called out, "Escape, escape, a great company of armed Romans is approaching!"

The boy had been appointed as look-out man. He had been able to survey a wide area from the summit of the mountain.

"The Romans are close, hardly a mile from here. They are approaching from several directions and are attempting to encircle the ruin."

"Then let us use the underground passage!" said Elazar.

Several youths lifted a slab of stone which had previously appeared to be firmly fixed in the ground, and all the youths descended into the passage. Shimon went first, followed by the boy, then Ithamar, followed by all the other youths, one after the other. Elazar came last. He laid down the slab of stone in such a way that it covered the major part of the opening and only allowed him the smallest possible space through which he could descend. After he had entered the passage, he lifted the slab with superhuman strength and pushed it back in its place. Now the youths found themselves in a long, dark passage. Suddenly, Ithamar caught sight of a glowing fire. Barak approached a basin which contained coal covered with ashes. Coals continue to glow for a long time if they are covered with ashes. The youths had deposited this basin of coal carefully in the underground passage in case of sudden attack. Barak blew away the ashes, a little flame leaped up, and he lit a torch of pitch from it. Now the dark passage became brighter, and they advanced further and further between the old subterranean walls. In this way the youths walked on for an hour or more, till they reached a door which Elazar unlocked, and locked again behind him after all the youths had reached a rocky cave from which they came into the open air.

"Before we leave the cave," said Elazar to his companions, "we must thank the All-Merciful that He allowed us to escape the present danger. Then let us take counsel and decide what to do now."

Elazar said in a loud voice, "Blessed art Thou, O Lord, our God, King of the universe, Who has saved us in a wonderful way!"

"Amen," they responded with one breath. "And now," Elazar continued, "we must decide where we shall go. But first we must find out how the Romans discovered our meeting, for it is obvious that the attack was well prepared and that only treason could have put the enemy on our tracks. Who among you, my brothers, was so careless as to entrust someone else with our secret?"

All remained silent. Ithamar was overcome by a sudden fear. He had taken Orev into his confidence. Since early childhood he had never had a secret from his father's steward. Could Orev be a traitor? Impossible! Orev, who loved him and his father so much and hated the Romans? It was quite unthinkable that Orev should have betrayed him and his companions. "I ask you, my brothers," continued Elazar after a short interval, "open your hearts to me, and if someone has entrusted our secret to his father or brother, sister or fiancée, even to his best friend, let him speak up, so that we may find out from where the betrayal came."

Again all remained silent.

"Then I must assume that the Romans heard of it in a way which remains a mystery to us. What shall we do now? Shall we disperse and return to the city from different directions? It is possible that every one of us will be arrested and imprisoned immediately."

Yehudah said, "My advice is that we first send someone out in order to find out exactly what our situation is. If our names are unknown in the enemy camp, he will come back to us and report that we can enter the city without fear. But if he does not return, we will know that he has been taken prisoner, and then the others can save themselves by escaping into the mountains. Surely it is better that only one suffers and not all of us. I am quite willing to risk my life and do what I have suggested, according to the dictum of the sages that he who makes a proposal should undertake its execution."

"Not so, Yehudah," replied Elazar. "Why should you endanger your life because you have offered us good advice? For your advice is good, and in my opinion your proposal is the best plan for us. Let us cast lots, as our fathers used to do in similar circumstances, and the youth on whom the lot falls shall go."

"Listen to me, my friends!" said Ithamar. "Please choose me as your messenger. I have entered your circle but this day, and we can be fairly certain that the Roman spies have no knowledge of my membership in the group. I shall be able to enter the city without arousing suspicion and find out whether they know the names of the individual zealots or not. Also, I am familiar with the procurator's palace. I went there only a few weeks ago in order to chat with a young Roman, a childhood friend of mine. I shall find ways and means of investigating this matter and communicate it to you."

"I cannot agree to your suggestion," said Yehudah. "Why should we choose you, who has joined us only today, to undertake this dangerous mission? It would be irresponsible and make us feel ashamed forever. Let the lot decide, and no matter on whom it falls, not excluding you, Ithamar, that person shall expose himself to the danger. I would like to mention another point here. Elazar must not take part in this lottery, since his opinions are too well known in Roman circles and his continued leadership is vital for the success of our movement. It would not matter much if one of us were captured by the Romans; even if all of us were killed, the loss would not be so important to our people. But Elazar alone is worth as much as a thousand brave men; his life must not be endangered. I think you will all agree with me in this respect."

"Certainly, definitely!" the youths responded.

"But I disagree with you," said Elazar. "I am no better than you, and my blood is not more red than yours."

His opposition was of no avail. His companions declared that they would all follow him on foot if he went up to Jerusalem now. After repeated pleas from his friends, Elazar finally acquiesced. Now he had to arrange the casting of the lots. With his eyes blindfolded, he approached one of the friends, touched him with his hand and called out the number one hundred and twenty. Then he removed the scarf from his eyes and counted, beginning with the youth whom he had touched with his hand and continuing to the right. He counted on and on, walking around the circle several times. The number one hundred and twenty fell on Ithamar.

"Ithamar, the lot has chosen you," said Elazar. "Go now, my friend, my brother! Our most ardent prayers will accompany you. May the God of our fathers protect you!"

XI

IN ENEMY HANDS

THE BOY YONATHAN ACCOMpanied Ithamar to the place where the mountain range came to an end and one could see the road leading up to Jerusalem.

As Ithamar walked by himself along the road, he remembered his father and his fiancée, and his heart became heavy. If he were to be arrested and cast into prison on entering the city, how would his father be able to bear this terrible pain? And what would be his own fate, what punishment would the enraged procurator impose on him? The Romans were hard and cruel. A human life meant nothing to them, and the death penalty was carried out daily in the countries under their rule. Deep in thought, he reached Tzofim, from where the city could be surveyed. There she lay, silent and at peace, the queen of cities. The Temple which the Lord had chosen as His resting place appeared before him in all its glory. He was still a free man; he could turn back and hide in one of the other cities of the land, or else he could join numerous other dissatisfied citizens and hide together with them in the mountain caves, safe from Roman persection. But no! That was impossible! He had promised his companions to risk entry into the city. First he had volunteered to go, and after this offer had been refused, the lot had chosen him to undertake this dangerous mission. He had to keep his word and fulfill his mission, even though it might cost him his life and cause his father and his fiancée great suffering. "My God," he said, "Thou art all-powerful and able to save me from the danger which threatens me, if that should be Thy will. My fathers trusted in Thee, they trusted and Thou didst save them. They implored Thee and they were saved; they believed in Thee and escaped from shame. I know full well that I am unworthy of a miracle. But Thou hast been my protector ever since I was born; me alone didst Thou keep alive of all my brothers and sisters. Save me now for the sake of my old father, lest he sink in grief into his grave; for the sake of my faithful bride, lest she waste away her young life in grief and pain. Do not remain distant from me, for danger is near and I have no helper except for Thee alone!"

After he had thus fortified himself through prayer, Ithamar descended the mountain briskly. Soon he reached the gate of the city and passed through unmolested. The Roman soldiers who were keeping guard took no notice of him at all. Ithamar rejoiced in his heart. Nobody followed him. Probably they did not know the names of the youths who had gathered in the mountain ruin, or else they did not know that he had joined the group. In spite of this he decided not to go back to his father's house immediately, but first to visit his fiancée's father, in order to be assured that there was no danger awaiting him.

When Ithamar entered the house of his future father-in-law, the latter met him with a cry of horror. "Unhappy Ithamar, where do you come from? Do you not know that the Romans are looking for you, that you are accused of having planned a rebellion! They went out in vain to capture you and your companions, and now you enter the lion's den of your own free will! They have already searched for you in your father's house. They have also examined every chamber and every cellar and loft in my house, because they suspected that you might be hiding here, while you walk about openly and freely in the streets of the city! Come along quickly; let me hide you until you find an opportunity to escape from the city and to flee to the mountains."

"How is my father? How did he receive the frightful news?"

"Your father has been arrested and thrown into prison. They want to keep him as a hostage until you are found."

Ithamar grew pale.

"My father," he murmured, "my old, weak and sick father in prison, and I am responsible for it! I must go to the Roman procurator immediately and give myself up to him, so that they will release my dear father."

"Foolish boy, you must not do that! They would condemn you to death and kill you, while they cannot do much harm to your father. The Romans know that

Elyakim has always kept himself aloof from all political affairs. They will release him in a few weeks' time, when they feel convinced that he does not know your whereabouts. Come along and follow me, that I may hide you as well as I possibly can."

"I cannot do that. I cannot let my father stay imprisoned. He is old, weak and sick, and a lengthy stay in prison would quickly lead to his death."

Tirtzah entered. "My daughter," her father called to her, "help me to bring your fiancé to his senses. This foolish lad first gets involved in dangerous schemes and now, when his plans have been discovered, intends to rush right into the lion's den, to certain death."

"Ithamar," said Tirtzah, crying, "what have you done? Did you not think of my grief and of your old father's pain?"

"Whatever I have done, my Tirtzah, I can justify fully before God. I know equally well that it is now my sacred duty to offer myself up to the Romans and to set my father free."

Tirtzah cried loudly in despair, "Then you are lost to me forever! Unhappy youth, you will not only bring about your own death, but also mine and that of your aged father. Elyakim will not survive the execution of his only child for long, and his gray head will sink into the grave in grief. And as for me, what good is my life to me, if you have been murdered? I shall end my days in mourning and pain, till the grave opens for me as well."

"Please don't make it more difficult for me, Tirtzah! I cannot act otherwise. If I had a thousand lives, I would sacrifice them gladly in order to shorten my father's stay in prison, even by one hour. As for you, Tirtzah, time will make you forget the unhappy Ithamar, and you will find comfort in the arms of a husband who is worthier than I."

"You do not love me as much as I love you, Ithamar. I have been accustomed to regarding you as the source of my future happiness. You are the light of my life, and if you should perish, there is neither hope nor joy for me."

She threw herself down before him and sobbed.

"I implore you to preserve your life for our sake and not to expose yourself to certain death," she said.

Ithamar could no longer keep back his tears.

"My precious bride," he said, crying, "I see now what a jewel I would have acquired if I had been privileged to bring you home as my wife. But still I am unable to do other than fulfill my duty. Joy would never smile on me again if the weak heartbeats which keep my father alive were to be extinguished in prison. Goodbye, my beloved; try to forget me! Perhaps God Almighty in His mercy will release me from the jaws of the lion and lead me back to my loved ones in joy and happiness."

With gentle determination he turned away from Tirtzah, stretched out his hand to her father and left the house. With firm steps, he hastened to the palace of the procurator.

XII

APPREHENSION

IN VAIN DID THE COMRADES wait for Ithamar's return. They spent the whole night in sadness and anxiety. "Perhaps it got too late for him to send us a message before the gates were closed," said Elazar. "Let us wait here quietly to hear what he has to tell us tomorrow morning."

The friends had stored food and drink in the cave for an emergency like this. Together they said the evening prayers, ate and drank, and then lay down to rest. But sleep escaped them, for they could not erase from their minds the thought of the unhappy fate which might have overtaken Ithamar, and that in such a case they would not be allowed to return home. The night appeared to be endless, and when dawn broke through the rift in the rock, the youths rose, left the cave and went to a nearby spring of water in order to wash and say their morning prayers. Then they had breakfast, and when they had eaten their fill, Elazar delivered a talmudical discourse. Meanwhile, it was almost noon, and no news had been received from Ithamar.

"Brothers," said Elazar, "I shall set out to discover the fate of our friend so that we can decide what we should do next."

"You stay here, Elazar," said Yehudah. "You are too well known to the Romans and will arouse suspicion. Probably they will search for you more than for any of us. I shall go out and attempt to find out what has become of our friend Ithamar. Today is Thursday, and this afternoon the farmers return from the weekly market. Perhaps I shall succeed in finding out what happened in Jerusalem by questioning the farmers."

"No," said Elazar, "I will never again delegate a dangerous mission to anyone. It is bad enough that Ithamar has perished through my fault."

"Do not talk like that!" replied Barak. "The lot has decided it and therefore it was the Lord's will. I, too, must raise my voice in protest against your going out to investigate, Elazar. You are too excitable and could easily endanger yourself and all of us. Yehudah is best suited to this task. He knows how to get into conversation with strangers in order to find out what he needs to know. Since our friend Yehudah has volunteered for this task, let him go. May God grant that he bring us back good news."

"Go with God, Yehudah," said Elazar. "May the All-Merciful bless your going out and your return from now and forevermore."

"Amen," the companions responded, and Yehudah departed. Soon he reached the road, but instead of walking towards Jerusalem, he turned in the direction of

Hebron. He progressed at a leisurely pace, confident that soon farmers on their way home from Jerusalem would catch up with him. He was not disappointed, for soon he heard steps approaching him from behind. He turned round and saw a young man with an empty basket on his head. Yehudah stopped and called to the approaching youth, "Peace be with you!"

"And peace be with you," replied the stranger.

"Perhaps it might please you, if we walked on our way together. Company is sweet and the road is long."

"You are quite right," said the farmer. "I, too, dislike walking along by myself. Usually my cousin Yochanan accompanies me, but today he was delayed by a legal dispute with his neighbor. The case will probably only be decided in the late afternoon and then poor Yochanan will be forced to spend the night in Jerusalem. I hope he will win his lawsuit."

"You should not wish for that! If he is right, our excellent judges will decide in his favor. If not, then we should not wish to see the law bent in his favor. You should rather say, 'May God enlighten the judges, that they decide as the law demands.' "

The farmer regarded the young wanderer in astonishment. "Who are you, that you speak to me like an angel of God?" he enquired. "Perhaps you are the prophet Eliyahu, who will be sent to announce the coming of the Redeemer who will free us from the yoke of Rome?"

"I am a man like you," the youth replied with a smile. "My name is Yehudah and I am a pupil of Rabban Gamliel."

"Rabban Gamliel, the holy man, the prince of Israel, whose wisdom is supposed to equal that of his father's, the unforgettable Hillel? If you are indeed the pupil of that man, I am not surprised at your wise words. We countrymen have so little contact with the sages of Israel. Thus I thank my good fortune which has led me to meet you, Rabbi Yehudah. My name is Yissachar, son of Yoash, of blessed memory, from Ein Parah, a village between Jerusalem and Hebron. My father has left me some fields and vineyards which I till together with my wife. Every Monday and Thursday I take the fruit and vegetables into town and sell them there. We live happily and contentedly, and our only wish is that the disgraceful yoke of Edom should be removed from our shoulders."

"Why do you complain so much about the yoke of Rome?"

"Esav's greed knows no limits, and the taxes imposed on us can hardly be paid. Whatsoever we save is taken from us by the tax collector, and those who could not save anything become poor, for Edom knows neither kindness nor mercy. But even greater than their greed is their brutality. Have you heard the story which has roused the anger of the whole of Jerusalem since yesterday?"

"I have been away from the city for a long time, so I have not heard what happened there."

"Have you heard of Elyakim, son of Chizkiyah?"

"Certainly, since he is one of the noblest and best men of our people."

"Well, this distinguished sage, who was once a pupil of the great Hillel, this father of the poor and counselor of widows and orphans, was thrown into prison and threatened with death."

"You alarm me! Perhaps you have also heard why they treated him in such a manner?"

"Elyakim has a son of seventeen or eighteen who is alleged to have planned a rebellion. They sent off three cohorts in order to capture the lad, and since the soldiers did not find him, they have thrown the old man into prison."

"Disgusting!"

"Listen, there is worse to come. The youth, quite an innocent lad, returned to the city without knowing anything, and there he was told of his father's imprisonment. The brave son hastened to give himself up to the procurator, who was touched by the noble courage of the youth and changed the death penalty, which had already been proclaimed, into service as a galley slave. Early this morning the lad was led away in bonds to a fate which is a thousand times worse than death."

Yehudah was completely shattered by the terrible news he had just heard. His knees felt weak and he walked with difficulty.

"I walk too fast for you," said Yissachar. "I shall walk more slowly."

Yehudah managed to regain his composure.

"Have there been other arrests?" he asked.

"None as far as I know. I accompanied my cousin to the Law Courts. The famous Chananyah ben Chizkiyah was to preside. He had not arrived yet, and they feared that he too might have been arrested by the Romans because of his son. When he finally did appear, everyone rushed towards him, kissing his hand or his gown and said, 'Blessed be the Lord Who has protected you.' At the same time, I heard that they had been afraid on account of many other great and respected men whose sons are rebels, but without cause—nobody has been arrested except Elyakim."

"Farewell, my friend," said Yehudah, stretching out his hand to the countryman. "Thank you for the pleasure of your company, but now my path leads to the left."

Without waiting for Yissachar's answer, he hastened to report to his companions what he had discovered.

XIII

ELYAKIM'S COMMAND

When Yehudah returned to his companions in the cave and told them what he had learned from the farmer, the young men were overcome with a deep sadness. Elazar, the strong man, whose heart was as brave as a lion's, cried over the fate of his beloved friend Ithamar, as once David had cried for Yonathan. He asked his comrades to hasten with him to Jaffa, in order to liberate their dear friend by force from the hands of the Roman soldiers. Soon he had to admit, however, that such an attempt would be foolish. Apart from the hopelessness of making any attempt against superior armed forces, it would have been much too late to succeed. They could be sure that Ithamar had already been brought on board a Roman vessel by now, and how could they even attempt to free him from there?

"Farewell, my brother Ithamar," cried Elazar at last. "Wherever you may be and whatever your suffering, you shall be called happy, for you have sacrificed yourself for your people! The good God will redeem you, or will give you ample reward in the life to come."

Now the companions had to consider what to do next. Apparently only Ithamar had been suspected, since only Elyakim had been arrested and no relative of any other youth. They decided to return separately to the city. Nobody paid any attention to them in Jerusalem, and they continued to remain unmolested.

When Elyakim returned to his desolate home, he was broken in body and spirit. Day and night he mourned his lost son. All his friends came to comfort him, yet he received nobody. But when the prince of Israel, the most respected Rabban Gamliel, came to bring comfort to his old friend and former fellow student, Elyakim could not turn him away.

"The Lord is just in all His ways and merciful in all His deeds!" Thus, in the words of the Psalmist, did the prince address the bereaved father.

"The Lord is just and full of love," the grieving father replied, "and we cannot know His ways, nor understand His deeds. The light of my eyes, my heart's joy, my most beloved son, my only one, has been taken away from me and cast into abject misery, and all that in order to free me from prison, where I had been thrown through no fault of my own. My son, my son, if only you had saved yourself, how gladly I would have died for you!"

"Your lament and sorrow are fully justified, and I have no hope of comforting you in your grief. Another matter brings me to you: namely, concern for your son's future."

"You, Rabban Gamliel, know well that my son has been sent to a place from which there is no return!"

"Nevertheless, it is possible that he may come back one day, though you may not live to see his return. If Almighty God decides that you should go the way of all flesh and be gathered to your fathers, the Romans will confiscate your property, regarding it as the inheritance of a condemned man. Even if they treat the matter favorably, your property will be divided among hundreds of distant relatives, and it will be practically impossible for your son to regain his property, should he one day return. Therefore I have come to advise you how to proceed, so that your son should not become a pauper if he ever returns."

"Not in vain do they praise your wisdom, my prince. In my deep grief, I have thought of nothing but my irreplaceable loss and the awful fate of my dear son. I would have spent the remaining days of my earthly life in useless lament and bitter complaint. But the Lord has given you divine wisdom, and you have taught me to consider an eventuality which is not entirely impossible, though it is not likely to arise."

"Can we be overheard here?"

"My steward, Orev, has traveled to Hebron, and there are only a few other servants in the house. Still, I shall first lock the doors of the adjoining rooms so that no one may surprise us."

Elyakim proceeded as he had said, and the two respected sages conversed together for a long time. Then the prince took leave of his friend. From then on, Elyakim seemed like a changed man, no longer entirely overwhelmed by his deep grief.

When Orev returned the next day, he noticed the change in his master. "The prince came to see you, my dear lord," he said to his master, "and I see with great joy that he has succeeded in relieving your mind."

"You are right, Orev. He has drawn my attention to the fact that I must make provisions for my house, draw up a legal testament and have it signed by the authorities. As you know, I have only distant relatives, and according to the usual law of inheritance, my fortune would be divided into hundreds of parts."

"I suppose he advised you to leave your entire fortune to charitable causes or to donate it to the treasury of the Temple?"

"We talked of it, but the prince did not advise me to do that. We are under Roman rule, and the Temple treasury is not safe from their hands. We agreed that I should leave my wealth to one person, so that my house may continue to practice charity as before. You, Orev, have always been a faithful servant to me. I am convinced that you will give to the poor with an open hand and will contribute generously to every good cause, just as I and my ancestors have done. In my will, I shall appoint you as heir to my entire fortune."

A triumphant smile lit up the face of the slave, and he would have called out in delight. But he quickly hid his emotions and fell down at his master's feet, embraced his knees and cried out, as if in tears, "My generous master, thank you for your kind thought. But it doesn't make me feel happy. I am filled with sadness because you cannot leave your property to your beloved son. How I would love to serve him, just as I have served you! But the unfortunate one will never return! I swear to you, however, with a holy oath, that I will administer your fortune in your own spirit. No hungry man shall leave this door unsatisfied, no unhappy man shall depart uncomforted. I shall support the pupils of the scholars generously and contribute to the care of the sick as much as it is in my power, and I shall help to support our oppressed brothers, as you have always done."

"Yes, Orev. Keep your oath and administer the large property, which will soon be yours, in this manner. Then the house of Elyakim will continue, and you will replace the lost son for me. Now go and call the wise Dosa for me, so that he can draw up my last testament and have it signed by witnesses and confirmed by the Roman authorities."

XIV

THE DESOLATE BRIDE

ELYAKIM DIED AND ALL OF Judah mourned him. He was laid to rest in the grave of his fathers, and when, at the funeral, Rabban Gamliel praised his great virtues, his learning, his charity, his unfailing subservience to the divine will, many tears were shed and all those present were touched by the unhappy fate of the deceased sage. But their mood changed suddenly when they heard that he had appointed his slave as his heir. They had expected the deceased to leave his fortune to his son, and in the event of his death, to charitable institutions. The fact that the Canaanite, as the steward was called by the people, would inherit a princely fortune was greatly resented. Many criticized the memory of the deceased. Others alleged that the old man could not have been fully responsible for his deeds, for otherwise he would not have made such a foolish bequest. Orev, too, heard some of these comments and laughed maliciously. But only for a moment. Then he resumed the mournful face and the bent attitude which he had assumed since his master's death. For seven days he sat on the earth and cried as if he had lost a father. He remained in deep mourning for thirty days and, whenever he met people, could only lament and weep at the great loss he had suffered through the death of his patriarchal friend and benefactor. But after this period, he discarded his mask and began to enjoy his great property. He dressed with extreme care and appeared wherever he could show himself off as a rich and noble man. He contributed to many charitable causes, provided his name would be mentioned in public as the generous donor. But it never occurred to him to do acts of kindness secretly, as Elyakim used to do. He treated the humble poor who relied on his assistance in a cold and harsh way.

Ever since Ithamar's great misfortune, Tirtzah spent her days in deep mourning. In vain did her father try to comfort her.

"My precious child," he said, "I cannot bear to see you so unhappy. Forget the unfortunate one who can hardly be counted any longer among the living. Who ever heard of a Roman galley slave returning to life and liberty? That dreadful form of slavery kills its unfortunate victims only too quickly. You must consider him as if he were already dead. You have mourned for him long enough. Open your heart to the joys of life once more. You are still young, and when you stop worrying, you will bloom once again in your full beauty. Though my fortune is not great, you are my only heiress, and our family is one of the noblest in Judah. The daughter of Elazar ben Zevulun from the house of

Azaryah, my daughter, will not lack suitors when she returns of her own free will to life and joy."

"I beg of you, my father," replied Tirtzah, "leave me alone and do not insist. I cannot forget my beloved Ithamar!"

"Then my family must come to an end, and I cannot expect to experience the great happiness of rocking grandchildren on my knees! My dear wife, your mother, is dead, and I am too old to marry again and expect to be blessed with children. Your mother and I remained childless for many years. My friends urged me to take yet another wife. But I loved your mother too much to be able to install a rival at her side. Then you were born to us, a latecomer, a child of our old age. You became our pride and joy, and when my friend and colleague Elyakim desired you for his son, we were the happiest of people. Your mother died and I felt comforted to see her image reproduced in you. You know how I have loved your fiancé, but I was not granted the joy of being present at your wedding. God has decided otherwise, His will be done!"

Crying bitterly, Tirtzah embraced her father.

"My dearest father," she said tearfully, "in addition to my deep grief, I feel sad at making you unhappy, but I cannot act differently. I have a feeling that Ithamar will return to us alive and well. How unhappy I would be then, if he found me married to another. How can I give my hand to another man when my heart belongs to the friend of my childhood! You are a wise man, my father, a pupil of Hillel the Great. Tell me, is it permitted to give oneself to a man when one carries the picture of another man in one's heart?"

"But I have asked you to forget that unfortunate man!"

"That is quite impossible for me, my father."

"You are right to a certain extent. Our sages teach us that only the dead are forgotten and not the living, as Yirmiyahu said, 'I have been forgotten from the heart like a dead man.' They say that a galley slave rarely survives the first year of slavery. Let us wait till the end of that year. Then you may succeed in removing his image from your heart."

"My father, what a sad prospect you offer me!"

"My child, my child, how can I leave you alone in this difficult period, a lonely, defenseless orphan, when it will please God to call me away from this life?"

"My father, how you do depress my spirits! Must I lose you as well?"

"That is the way of the world, my dear child. The old are laid to rest in the grave, and the young ones take their place. Therefore I want you to marry a man who will stand by your side and protect you. We live in sad times. We suffer under the yoke of the Romans, and Judah finds it hard to bear this heavy yoke. There is unrest among the people everywhere, and the time must be near when the Jewish lion will attempt to cast off the yoke of Esav. Then all existing foundations will be shaken, and then, when I lay down my tired head to be gathered to my fathers, who shall protect you, my poor, defenseless child?"

"The Father of orphans will not desert me. Esther was an orphan, with neither father nor mother, but God protected her, and she became the savior of her people. Do not worry about me, Father. All-Merciful God will grant us that you may remain with me for a long, long time to come and live to see Ithamar's return, so that you can hand over your only child to the son-in-law whom you chose long ago and rejoice with us on our wedding day."

"May God grant it, but..."

"Do not open your mouth with a foreboding of harm, Father."

Tirtzah kissed her father's hand and looked into his eyes wistfully before leaving him to attend to her domestic duties. Her father stayed in his room. He took a scroll of parchment from his cupboard in order to study from it and sighed deeply. He was worried about the future of his child and of his people. He forced himself to read the parchment scroll unrolled before him. It was the Book of Psalms in which he had often found peace and comfort. He found the twenty-seventh Psalm and read in a loud voice: "O Lord, my light and my salvation, whom shall I fear? O Lord, Thou art the stronghold of my life, of whom shall I be afraid?" And when he came to the tenth verse, "For though my father and my mother forsake me, the Lord will gather me up," his heart shared his daughter's hope, and he fervently recited the concluding verse of the Psalm, "Hope in the Lord, be strong and let your heart take courage and hope in the Lord!"

"Hope in the Lord," repeated the father, tortured by fear and anxiety. "Hope in the Lord. Even if things appear hopeless, be strong and let your heart be firm. For the God of Israel is omnipotent. Hope in Him alone, and He will let you attain the fulfillment of your hope."

XV

THE LOAN

One day, after the year of mourning for Elyakim was over, Orev appeared before Tirtzah's father with a grave demeanor. "Permit me," he said, "to resume the old connections of my dear, unforgettable master. His friends are also my friends. The man he loved can be sure of my love and admiration. A few weeks before his death, he said to me, 'My dear Orev, I appoint you my heir, so that you may continue to conduct my household as I have done.' You will have heard, friend of my beloved master, that I try to dispense charity to the poor as Elyakim used to do. I should like to continue the traditions of the house whose owner I have become in other respects as well. Your daughter was destined for the unfortunate son of my master. I wish her to become the mistress of all the wealth which Elyakim has left me. Grant me your Tirtzah as my wife!"

Tirtzah's father shook with rage. He considered it a great insult that the former slave should presume to ask for the hand of the daughter of Elazar ben Zevulun of the house of Azaryah. For he derived his descent from the royal prince Azaryah who had once chosen to be cast into the fiery furnace, together with his companions, Chananyah and Misha'el, rather than bow down before Nevuchadnetzar's idol. Now this man, whose parents, grandparents and great-grandparents had been slaves, had the impudence to court Tirtzah, who was of royal descent! He would have liked to give the former slave a sharp rejoinder, or at least to show him the door without a reply. However, Orev was now rich and respected, and gave alms to the poor, and Elazar therefore tried to suppress his rising anger.

"My dear Orev," he said, "I am obliged to you for your kind proposal to make my daughter the mistress of your great wealth. You have a certain claim to aspire to Tirtzah's hand, since you have taken the place of the unfortunate Ithamar. Yet, Tirtzah daily awaits the return of her unfortunate bridegroom and refuses to consider any other match."

"Who has ever returned to freedom from the galleys?"

"I know, but the human heart is foolish and often clings to hopes that cannot come true."

"Then I shall wait until she feels certain that her hopes are in vain. Perhaps we will hear news of Ithamar's death."

Elazar regarded the former slave with distaste. Such is the love this man professes to feel for his master and his master's son, he thought. Orev noticed the angry expression and guessed Elazar's thoughts.

"What do you want?" he said. "Why should I not desire his death? Is it not better to die than to be chained to the rowing bench? Still, let us not quarrel, but tell me that I am acceptable to you as a son-in-law."

"Do not insist on such an assurance from me. It would be useless anyhow as long as Tirtzah absolutely refused to become engaged to any other man."

Orev cast a look of open hatred at Elazar. It was clear to him now that this man of modest means refused to give him his daughter as a wife, despite the fact that he was one of the wealthiest men in the land. In his heart he thought that the time for revenge would come. Aloud, however, he said, "As you like, Elazar. I shall wait and ask you again later on." He left the house, full of hatred and anger.

At that time, the Roman procurator, Valerius Gratius, had been recalled to Rome. The emperor, Tiberius, stood at the head of the Roman Empire, but he ruled in name alone, for the real ruler of the great empire was Lucius Aelius Sejanus, the emperor's favorite. He had removed most of the emperor's relatives by poisoning them—among them Drusus, the appointed heir to the throne—and had persuaded the emperor himself to settle permanently on the island of Capri, so that he, as Tiberius's deputy, could rule the empire. Sejanus, in his turn, had favorites whom he provided with the most lucrative positions. Thus Valerius Gratius was recalled from Judea, and Pontius Pilatus was appointed in his place. As soon as the latter arrived in Caesarea, which was the seat of the Roman procurator of Judea, he increased the burdens imposed on the Jewish people to an extent unequaled by any of his predecessors. He demanded that the Jews should set up images of the emperor and pay divine homage to them in the manner of the other nations ruled by Rome. A cry of disgust passed through the whole of Judea when the images were brought up to Jerusalem. The most noble and distinguished citizens hastened to Caesarea in order to intercede with the procurator and implore him to desist from this fearful request. The procurator refused to receive the deputations and locked the gates of his palace against them. For five days the men of Judea surrounded the palace. On the sixth day, Pilatus ordered his legions to advance and remove the petitioners by force. The Roman soldiers rushed towards the Jews with drawn swords and ordered them to leave the place. Then Berachyahu, a brother to Elazar ben Zevulun, advanced and said to his fellow Jews:

"Brethren, let us not move from this place even one hair's breadth. Let the Romans see that we men of Judah are ready to lay down our lives in order to sanctify the name of the one God. Brethren, I am a descendant of Azaryah, who allowed himself to be cast into the fiery furnace because he refused to bow down before Nevuchadnetzar's idol. Let us follow the example of our great forefathers and sacrifice our lives for the sanctification of the Divine Name. I am ready to die!"

"Hail to you, ben Azaryah," they shouted on all sides. "We too prefer to die rather than be forced to kneel before images made of wood and stone and sacrifice to them."

The legions were about to strike with drawn swords when Pilatus, out of admiration for the courage of the Judeans, ordered the soldiers to withdraw. He also revoked his decree and promised to have the statues removed immediately from Jerusalem. Thus Judea escaped from a great danger.

When Berachyahu returned to Jerusalem, he was received by the people with great rejoicing. Then his emotions led him to utter a thoughtless word. "Brethren," he said to those assembled before him, "this time danger has been removed, thanks to God's mercy. But how easily can such events be repeated! Judah will be unable to serve God in peace, unless the uncircumcised cease to rule over us as masters."

The new procurator, wishing to discover the mood of the people, had ordered some of his officials to mingle among the crowds, disguised as Jews. These men overheard Berachyahu's words, and as soon as he returned home, he was arrested and taken to prison. Not long after this, Pilatus himself arrived in Jerusalem. Elazar ben Zevulun hastened to him in order to beg for the release of his brother. The procurator replied in a mocking tone, "You Judeans are so ready to sacrifice your lives; now let me see whether you are equally prepared to give away your money. If you give me five thousand pieces of silver, I will release your brother!"

Elazar left him. Then he met Orev who enquired as to the success of his petition. When Elazar told him of the procurator's demand, Orev said:

"Elyakim would surely have lent you this sum. I

follow his example in every respect. Come home with me and I will lend you the money."

"And how am I to pay it back?"

"You will easily persuade your numerous friends to collect the sum."

Elazar ben Zevulun was concerned only with the thought of setting his noble brother free. He therefore went with Orev, received the money, and gave him a promissory note. An hour later, Berachyahu was released from prison.

XVI

TRAPPED

The two brothers, Elazar and Berachyahu, made great efforts to collect sufficient money from their friends and acquaintances in order to repay their debt to Orev, but all their endeavors were in vain. The wealthiest citizens of Jerusalem belonged to the Sadducee sect from whom the pious brothers could neither wish nor expect any financial assistance. The small number of wealthy Pharisees were constantly burdened with so many obligations that they were unable to make large contributions. When Orev heard of these futile attempts at raising money, he sent the following message to Elazar ben Zevulun, "Do not bother about the repayment of your debt. I do not need the money and gladly allow you a longer period to repay me."

Another two years went by, and Tirtzah still refused every offer of marriage with great firmness. Then Orev appeared one day and said:

"I am sorry to have sad news for you. You may have heard that many daring pirates have been causing unrest for some time on the seas and along the coast. They have captured ships and robbed, burned and plundered the coast. Some time ago, the emperor equipped and armed a fleet and sent it to fight the pirates. A great naval battle took place, and the Romans were victorious. Most of the pirates' fleet was destroyed; the rest dispersed. However, the Roman fleet also suffered great losses. The battleship Juno was so badly damaged by the pirates that all the crew were drowned. On this ship, Ithamar, the unhappy son of my former master, was a galley slave."

Tirtzah began to weep violently.

"My Ithamar, my beloved bridegroom, whose return I awaited every hour...did you have to end your life in such a terrible way!?" she cried. "My happiness and my life lie buried in the sea; hungry sea monsters have devoured your body! If only I could have died instead of you!"

Elazar made no attempt to comfort her. He, too, was deeply grieved, and tears flowed from his eyes.

"My poor Elyakim," he said, "thus has your family been extinguished forever. Where did you hear this sad news, Orev?"

"The procurator arrived here from Caesarea yesterday. He had received the news directly from Rome. One of his officials, who is an acquaintance of mine, brought me this painful message."

Orev departed, leaving Tirtzah and her father in deep mourning. Next day, a man called Symmachos came to Elazar ben Zevulun and said:

"I have an offer for you, master. The rich and highly

respected Orev, whose charity and piety are generally admired, sends me to you in order to ask you for the hand of your only daughter."

"Why have you undertaken such a mission, Symmachos?" Elazar replied. "Do you not know that mine is one of the noblest families of Judah, that we are descendants of David, and of royal blood? How could I let my daughter marry a former slave?"

"What use is your former nobility? It will not prevent you from having to sit in prison. Take care not to provoke Orev! You have placed yourself in his power, since he possesses a promissory note from you which you cannot redeem, and which enables him to have you incarcerated in the debtor's prison at any time. Orev is highly regarded by the Roman procurator, whose favor he has won through rich presents. If you tell him that you despise him as a former slave, his anger will be aroused. You, as one of the sages of Israel, should know the words of the wise king: 'A debtor is a slave to his creditor.' Orev will have you imprisoned, and if you cannot pay, your property will be sold. But since the proceeds of such a sale would not cover the great sum you owe him, you yourself will have to be sold into slavery, even if only for six years. Orev will acquire you for himself, and you, the descendant of David, will have to serve the former slave!"

The unfortunate sage listened to these words and grew pale as death. He tried to speak but his tongue seemed paralyzed.

"You asked me why I agreed to bring you this offer,"

Symmachos continued. "You ought to know then that I agreed because I am your friend, and love and admire you. Orev wanted to approach you himself, but I prevented him, fearing you might offend him and bring about your own downfall. Think it over, Elazar. Orev, though a former slave, is now considered the equal of any man in Israel. Besides, he is rich and generous, and lives strictly according to the Law. You remember what the sages teach us, 'If your daughter is ripe for marriage, set your bondservant free and take him as your son-in law.' What is to become of your daughter if your property is sold and you are degraded into slavery? No youth of Israel will want to marry her then. But if you accept Orev's hand in friendship, he is prepared to return your promissory note to you immediately. Joy, happiness and wealth are offered to you on the one hand, shame and disgrace on the other. You must choose! I leave you now, but I will return tomorrow to hear your answer."

Symmachos went home, and Elazar remained alone. He stared in front of him with tears flowing from his eyes, which he neither noticed nor dried. Thus his daughter found him.

"What is the matter, Father?" she cried. "What new misfortune has befallen us?"

"A great misfortune, my child. Orev, Elyakim's former slave, wants to force me to give you to him as a wife. I am in his power. My promissory note gives him the power to sell my property and to make me his slave. He cannot do that according to Jewish law, but he has bribed the Roman procurator, so that the Roman authorities will do whatever he demands."

"What do you intend to do, Father?"

"I shall suffer any misfortune rather than force you, a daughter of the House of David, to marry a former slave."

"But I will not allow your gray head to be covered with disgrace. I will not allow you, my beloved father, to suffer such appalling misery. Since it is in my power to protect you, I shall not hesitate for a moment to do what my love for you and my duty as a daughter demand."

"You would...?"

"Did my unforgettable Ithamar not act exactly in the same way? Did he not sacrifice himself in order to set his old father free? For me, all happiness is over. I should have preferred to spend my days in lament and mourning for the dear friend of my youth, but now it is my sacred duty to protect my beloved father from shame and misery."

"God bless you, my beloved child! Truly you deserve a better fate. Still, this seems to be God's will. His will be done!"

Next day, when Symmachos brought Orev the message that father and daughter had agreed to the match, the former slave's joy knew no bounds. He had attained all his desires. He had supplanted Ithamar, whose wealth had now become his own property. He had also won the beautiful Tirtzah, whom he had always longed to possess. He cried out in elation, "I have reached the summit of the mountain. Who can cast me down to the ground?"

XVII

THE WARSHIP

DEAR READER! WE MUST NOW show you a dismal sight. Come and follow us to a Roman trireme.

To an observer, seeing it moving smoothly through the water, the trireme presents a most delightful picture. Its many oars move to and fro through the water with a regular rhythm, in perfect unison. But if we board the ship and go below deck, we see a sad scene. To the right and to the left, chained to their places in three long rows along each side of the ship, sixty slaves are pulling at the oars, while the supervisors stand over them with whips and urge them on. The oarsmen in the first and second rows are seated, while those in the third row have longer oars and stand. A lead weight is attached by a piece of shiny leather to the upper end of each oar, to ensure smooth motion. But great skill is needed in handling the oars, for otherwise a sudden wave may come and knock over a careless slave, throwing him head over heels into the sea. Only a little light penetrates through a lattice-work from the deck. Oral communication is not allowed.

Day by day the condemned men take their places without speaking one word. While they work, they are unable to see one another's faces, only the sweating back of the slave directly in front. Sleep and food fill the few permitted intervals. One never sees any oarsman laugh, nor hears the unfortunate slaves sing. What use is the tongue to a man, if it can only serve to express his sighs? The life of these wretches is like an underground stream, flowing slowly but steadily towards its exit, wherever that may be. Almost every nation is represented on the rowing benches. There you may find Britons, Lybians, Lombardians, Jews, Roman criminals, Scythians, Ethiopians, Greeks, and barbarians from the most distant lands. The activity of rowing is insufficient to occupy their minds, however primitive and simple they may be. The movements soon become automatic, even when the sea is stormy. As a result of their long slavery, the poor wretches become dull. Their obedience is spiritless and automatic. They live in the past and cannot imagine any future for themselves. In the course of time, their state of misery becomes a part of them.

In one such trireme sat the tribune, the ship's captain, thinking over many things. When the slaves' regular movements became boring to him, his attention turned to the individual oarsmen. These were never called by their names. Numbers affixed to the seats were used to identify the occupants. The tribune's sharp eye moved from bench to bench and rested at last on number sixty. The occupant of that seat was naked except for his loincloth, just like all his fellow slaves. He was young, apparently not much more than twenty years old. His youth did not rouse the tribune's pity, but his noble build, the perfection of the protruding muscles and his whole figure roused his admiration. He flattered himself on being an expert on this subject, since he had made a special study of physical perfection in the Palaesha, the fighting schools of Rome. "By the gods," he said to himself, "I like that man. He looks promising. I must find out more about him." At that moment the oarsman turned his face towards him. "A Jew," the tribune exclaimed, "and not much more than a boy." The Jew blushed under the tribune's gaze. He hesitated a moment with his oar, and the hammer of the supervisor came down on the table. He pulled himself together, turned his face away and applied himself to his work with renewed vigor. Later, when he looked again towards the tribune, he was surprised by the kind smile which greeted him. Meanwhile, the ship entered the straits of Messina, passed the city of Messina and continued eastwards, leaving the smoky clouds of Etna behind. Whenever the tribune returned to his observation post, his gaze returned to the oarsman, and he said to himself, "He is not like the others. Once a Jew did me a good turn. I must enquire about him!"

"Do you know the man who has just got up from the bench?" he asked the supervisor, when a change of oarsmen was taking place.

"Number sixty?"

"Yes!"

The supervisor looked at the oarsman. "As you

know," he said, "the ship only left the builders' yard a month ago. The crew is as strange to me as the ship."

"He is a Jew," the tribune remarked.

"The noble Serranus has a sharp eye."

"He is young," the tribune continued.

"But he is our best oarsman," the supervisor replied.

"I have often noticed the oar almost break in half from the power of his arm. What kind of temperament has he?"

"He is obedient. I don't know anything else. Once he asked me a favor."

"What was that?"

"He asked to be employed on the right side and on the left equally."

"Did he give a reason for the request?"

"He remarked that men who always work on the same side become deformed. Further, he explained that one day, in a storm or in battle, there could be an urgent need for him to change sides and then he would be incapable of fulfilling the task."

"Really? That is a new idea. What else have you noticed about him?"

"He is cleaner than his fellow slaves."

"He is like a Roman in that respect," said the tribune approvingly. "Do you know anything of his background?"

"Not a thing."

The tribune pondered a moment. Then he turned back to his seat and said, "Should I be on deck when he is relieved, send him to me. He should come alone."

About two hours later, Serranus sat beneath the ship's flag in a mood of expectancy—a mood in which, according to the teachings of philosophy, a well-disciplined mind remains perfectly calm. The man at the wheel sat in his usual place. Some of the ship's crew were asleep in the shadow of the sails. At the top of the mast sat a watchman. When Serranus raised his eye from the solarium, the sundial which indicated the direction in which they were going, he saw the oarsman approaching him.

"The supervisor told me that you wished to see me. Here I am."

Serranus looked with admiration at the slim, muscular figure before him, a figure which reminded him of the arena. But the young man's manner had also another effect—the tone of his voice indicated that he had spent his earlier life in a refined atmosphere; his gaze was curious, rather than defiant; he did not lose his poise under the tribune's scrutiny and showed no inclination to voice any complaint; neither defiance nor threat, but only a deep sadness seemed to envelope him. In unconscious acknowledgment of these favorable qualities, the Romans did not speak to him as a master to his slave, but rather like an older man to his younger equal.

"The supervisor tells me you are his best oarsman."

"It was kind of him to say that."

"Have you been serving for a long time?"

"About three years."

"At the oars?"

"I haven't left them for a day."

"That is hard work. Few men can continue rowing for more than a year without succumbing—and you are still a boy!"

"The noble tribune forgets that will power can strengthen the power of perseverance, and often enables a weak man to bear what would have defeated the powers of the strong."

"According to your speech you are a Jew."

"My ancestors were Hebrews long before the first Romans."

"The pride of your nation is also evident in you. What reason have you to be proud?"

"I am a Jew."

Serranus smiled. "Why have you been sent here?" he asked.

"I was accused of having planned a rebellion in order to break the dominion of Rome."

"You? Only a lad? Strange. What is your name?"

"Ithamar, the son of Elyakim."

A deep emotion flashed across the features of the tribune. But he controlled his feelings and said, "You may go now!"

XVIII

OUT OF BONDAGE

ITHAMAR WAS AGAIN SITting on the rowing bench. A ray of light had suddenly penetrated the dark night of his sad and monotonous life. He had neither recognized the tribune nor remembered even having seen him before, nor had he heard his name. Nevertheless, the mere fact that the tribune had actually called him, that the all-powerful ruler of the ship, the distinguished Roman, had deigned to enquire about his descent and his name, was sufficient to arouse great excitement in the unfortunate youth. What did the tribune intend to do with him? Perhaps Ithamar could expect to regain his freedom through him, for otherwise, why had the tribune taken this interest in him? For three long years now, Ithamar had worked as an oarsman, and during that period, he had repeatedly been moved from one ship to another. But no ship's officer had ever bothered to look at him, let alone talk to him. The ships traveled the seas, while the galley slaves had not the faintest idea of their destination. If a naval battle was about to be fought, the galley slaves were first tied to their benches, so that they could not mutiny while the battle was in progress. Anyone condemned to the galleys for life abandoned all hope. The monotony of the mechanical task made thought impossible. Suddenly, there was a glimmer of hope which revived his memories of the past. From an atmosphere of joy and happiness, Ithamar had been cast into the deepest night and misery. On that fateful day long ago, when he had entered the palace of the Roman procurator, he had been seized immediately, put in chains and cast into prison. The only thing that gave him comfort was the news that Valerius Gratius had given orders to set old Elyakim free. Early next morning, he himself had been taken to Jaffa under military escort, without any trial or examination. There he was put on board a trireme, dressed in the clothes of a slave and chained to a rowing bench. Ever since, he had traveled the seas, to the north and to the south, to the east and to the west. He did not come to know the countries which the ship passed by, for, even when the trireme lay anchored in the harbor, the galley slaves were not allowed on shore. They were only allowed to leave one ship in order to be led on board another. Such a life dulled the spirit and killed the imagination, and even memories die when all hope dies. Now a ray of hope had entered Ithamar's mind and aroused memories of the past. What had become of his old father? Had grief for his lost son killed him? What had become of Tirtzah? Had she forgotten the friend of her youth and given her hand to another man? Ithamar had nobody left in the world. He could not hope to find his old, feeble father alive, even if he should eventually regain his freedom. He could not expect that Tirtzah would remain faithful to a man who was bound to die soon. As to Orev, the youth felt as if a knife was turning in his heart when he remembered his father's steward. Had Orev been a traitor? He could not be certain. And what of his dear companions, Elazar, Barak, Yehudah and the others? Had they too been captured, or were they able to escape? Ithamar had not heard any news of their fate. He had not thought of the past for a long time, and now the figures of his loved ones reappeared before his eyes. If only he could see them again in real life, if only he could return to his beloved homeland and observe again the sacred commandments of Almighty God! A sincere prayer rose from his heart to his Father in Heaven, and his eyes filled with tears, while his arm continued to pull at the heavy oar.

The tribune, who was almost as excited as Ithamar, had remained on deck. He, too, had not recognized the youth immediately, and it was only the mention of his name that made him realize that this galley slave had once saved his life. He would gladly have set him free at once, but his power did not extend that far. Furthermore, he could not spare the best oarsman of his ship. He had a difficult task to fulfill. The Artenisis, as the ship was named, was the leading ship of a large flotilla and was followed at a close distance by a hundred other triremes. Serranus was the commander of the entire fleet. He had been ordered to clear the seas of pirates from all parts of the great Roman Empire who had joined forces to make these seas dangerous to cross. The pirates had aroused terror along the Roman Empire's long coastline. They would land suddenly in a harbor to rob and plunder the coastal districts, stealing cattle and all else that was valuable. They also carried men and women away as captives, to sell them as slaves on another coast. Eventually, the outcry from the many terror-stricken victims of these raids reached Rome. Furthermore, a number of Roman cargo ships bringing corn, fruit, gold, silver and costly cloths to Rome had been attacked and captured by the pirates. The warships which had been sent to protect them were put to flight by the superior power of the robbers. They reported that the pirates' fleet consisted of more than sixty triremes. The emperor had therefore ordered a strong fleet to be equipped and had appointed the tribune Anejus Serranus as its commander. Now the Romans planned to destroy the pirates, but first they had to discover their present whereabouts.

Suddenly, the fleet encountered a Roman warship, which together with two other warships was to have accompanied a merchant vessel to Rome. The pirates had captured the merchant vessel, but the warships had escaped. Now Serranus knew where to look for the pirates. He forgot the oarsman from Judea and had no interest in anything but the pursuit and defeat of the enemy whom he hoped to encounter very soon.

On deck, a statue of Artemis was erected with an altar in front of it. The tribune prepared to offer a sacrifice to ensure the mercy and protection of the goddess. First they brought a young pig which they slaughtered and burned. Then, large amounts of incense were thrown on the flames. The marines put on their armor. Great heaps of spears, javelins and arrows were piled up. Oil, baskets of cottonwood and other highly inflammable materials were prepared, and the galley slaves were chained to their benches. Every seat was provided with a chain and a heavy foot-iron. Each galley slave had to put his foot in the iron, and the chain was then locked. The unfortunate slaves could only obey silently. In case of accident, they had no way of escape.

Evening approached and the ship's lanterns were lit. The tribune had lain down to rest. Then, one of the sailors who had been on watch approached the fleet commander's couch and woke him up. Silently, the tribune rose, put on his helmet and went on deck. There the officers were already assembled, and the marines came up, one after the other. Then a trumpet sounded, and others joined in. There was a terrible turmoil. The catapults hurled heavy stones against the pirate ships. Fiery balls flew in both directions. Suddenly, there was a triumphant cry, for the Romans had driven one of the ships aground. But victory was not yet theirs. At times the Romans appeared to have the upper hand, and sometimes the pirates seemed to be gaining ground. At times, the sighs and desperate shouts of the drowning pirates could be heard, and sometimes bleeding and mortally wounded Romans were carried down below. The terrible battle lasted through the night until noon the next day. At last the pirate fleet was defeated, and only a few ships managed to escape. Most of the others were either sunk, or damaged and captured. Serranus and the Romans had won a decisive victory.

The victorious tribune now gave orders to pursue the escaping pirates. He then ordered the supervisor to release the galley slaves from their chains and to send number sixty to him.

"Ithamar," the tribune said to the young man, as he drew near, "you will not return to the rowing bench. I shall soon travel to Rome and will then ask the emperor to release you. After the great victory I have won, he will not refuse me this request."

Overcome with joy, Ithamar wished to throw himself at the Roman's feet. But the latter caught him in his arms and cried, "Come to my heart, my brother, savior of my life!"

XIX

THE BETRAYAL IS REVEALED

THE VICTORIOUS ANNIHILATOR of the pirates was received in Rome with great jubilation, and Sejanus, acting on the emperor's behalf, overwhelmed him with honor and gifts. Through his kind intervention, Ithamar now regained his liberty. However, he had to give a firm promise that he would never again conspire against the Roman Empire or fight against it. Ithamar had much difficulty in making up his mind to give this promise.

"My young friend," Serranus said to him, "if you refuse to give this promise you will again be chained to the rowing bench and thus be lost to the service of your people anyway."

"But how shall I act towards my old friends?" Ithamar replied. "Shall I stand by passive when the battle commences? I could not bear to do that."

"I shall make a suggestion to you. Your father will probably have died by now, his fortune confiscated, and your former bride will have married another. Poor and lonely, you would surely feel unhappy in your old surroundings, especially as you will be unable to mix again with your former friends. It so happens that I own large estates in Spain. There is a little town nearby called Toledo, which was founded by emigrants from Judea. I shall make you a present of one of those estates. Move to Spain and settle down there! Since many Judeans live there already, you will also be able to live according to your laws."

"I am very grateful to you, noble Serranus, for your generous offer. I do not wish to accept or reject it at present; first I must see what the conditions are like in Jerusalem."

Then Ithamar made the promise required of him and prepared for his departure. Serranus provided him with all necessities. Eight days later, a ship was to leave Brindisi for Jaffa. Ithamar used this interim period in order to acquaint himself with the great capital of the empire. One day, a centurion, a Roman captain, approached him, calling out from afar, "Salve amice! Greetings, my friend! I had not expected to meet you here!"

Ithamar regarded the captain with astonishment.

"Caius Cimber!" he exclaimed. "I would hardly have recognized you. You have already become a captain!"

"I told you four years ago in Jerusalem that Mars favors me. I have fought many fierce battles and found opportunities to distinguish myself. But now you must tell me how you come to be in Rome and whether you intend to stay here. If you have the time, please come home with me."

The friends went off together, and Ithamar told him all that had happened to him. When he had finished, Caius said, "My poor friend, how sad your fate has been. I, too, feel partly to blame for your misfortune, since it was I who aroused your ambition, or rather your patriotism, to a burning flame! Did they really condemn you without examination or trial? There is some mystery behind this which is worth investigating. Valerius Gratius is in Rome at the moment. As you know, I am acquainted with him and his family. I shall try to investigate the matter and inform you of the results."

The next day Cimber came to see his childhood companion again in the house of Serranus.

"Ithamar," he said, "I am able to enlighten you on everything. But first you must swear not to disclose to noble Serranus what I am about to tell you, nor to use it in order to harm the former procurator of Judea in any way. Valerius Gratius is an old friend of my family, and I do not wish him to suffer any unpleasantness because of me."

"I promise faithfully not to make any such use of your communications to me."

"Then listen! The former procurator of Jerusalem was in urgent need of money, a large sum of money, for he planned to return to Rome soon and to stand for the consulate. A man who wants to become a consul, however, must canvass for the votes of the citizens by providing lavish feasts and distributing generous presents. The simplest way of raising the required sum of money would have been through imposing new and heavy taxation. Thus, Valerius Gratius could have forced the Judeans to provide the financial means for the fulfillment of his plans. But there were great obstacles that prevented him for carrying out this simple plan. The procurator of Syria, the immediate superior of the procurators of Judea, was his personal enemy, and he would gladly have lent his ear to any Judean complaint and thus endanger Valerius Gratius's position. Then your faithful steward, Orev, appeared one day before the procurator and promised him ten thousand golden coins if he agreed to destroy you. He divulged the information you had given to your trusted servant, and the procurator felt entitled to accept the money in order to destroy an enemy of his country, a rebel. Three cohorts were dispatched to arrest you and your companions in your hideout, but you escaped in time. Then your beloved Orev advised the procurator to throw your father into prison. He was convinced that the son would then come forward voluntarily, and that is just what happened. Your father was released from prison, and, on Orev's evidence, you were condemned to death. But the Roman was more humane than your father's servant. The fact that you were willing to die in order that your father should be released from prison moved him greatly, and he granted you your life."

"A nice gift, the life of a galley-slave!"

"Still, you are now free!"

"But tell me, Caius, from where did Orev take all that money?"

"He stole it from your father."

"When I return I shall hold him to account for that."

"But remember your promise. No harm must come to the former procurator through these revelations. And now, my friend, introduce me to the noble Serranus. I have not yet had the good fortune of meeting the great man in person."

Ithamar led his friend into the tribune's chamber.

"Permit me, noble tribune, to introduce to you my childhood friend, the centurion, Caius Cimber," he said. "Though he is a brave warrior himself, he wishes to express his admiration to the greatest Roman hero of the seas."

"The fact that he is your friend, my Ithamar," Serranus said kindly, "recommends him to me even more than his youthful leadership of a cohort." With these words, he shook hands with the young man.

Cimber replied, "How fortunate I am that I am allowed to approach the great hero of the sea battle!"

XX

RETURN TO JERUSALEM

WHEN ITHAMAR TOOK LEAVE of his illustrious friend and powerful benefactor, Serranus said to him, "My young friend, I foresee that many difficulties lie ahead of you in your homeland if you attempt to reclaim your paternal inheritance. I have therefore thought fit to pave the way for you. The present procurator of Judea, Pontius Pilatus, owes his high position to mighty Sejanus. Therefore, I have obtained a letter of recommendation for you to the procurator of Judea. Here, take this letter. It will guarantee you the assistance of the Roman authorities in all matters."

"I thank you, noble Tribune," Ithamar replied, accepting the letter. "This recommendation, which I owe to your kind intervention, will surely be of great use to me."

Ithamar attempted to kiss the hand of his noble friend, but the tribune drew him close and embraced and kissed him.

"A happy journey to you, my young friend," he said. "May the God of your fathers protect you in all your ways. Do not forget that in Serranus you possess a friend who is always ready to serve you. Do not forget that I have offered you a home in Spain, in case you cannot remain in Jerusalem."

"I shall always remember you with the greatest affection and gratitude. May the God of my fathers protect you as well, and lead you to the highest pinnacles of fame."

After an uneventful voyage, Ithamar disembarked in Jaffa. He fell to the ground and kissed the holy soil of his homeland. He would gladly have remained in Jaffa and made enquiries at his country estate about the welfare of his father and Tirtzah. But he was overcome by a strong desire to see his loved ones again, and every moment of delay seemed a waste of time. Serranus had supplied him generously with money. He bought himself a mule and departed immediately for Jerusalem. On his journey, he considered whom to visit first in his home town. Since he had heard in Jaffa that Pontius Pilatus was at present staying in Jerusalem, he decided to see the procurator first and to hand him the letter of recommendation. In this way, any possible intrigues against him by Orev would be nipped in the bud. Next, he planned to visit Tirtzah and her father and to hear from them whether his father was still alive and only then would he enter his father's house.

When Ithamar reached the mountain peak from where Jerusalem could first be seen, he dismounted from his mule, fell to the ground and wept as he said, "Blessed art Thou, Lord our God, King of the universe, Who has kept us alive and preserved us and let us reach this time."

In Jerusalem, he went to an inn near the Jaffa gate and had a quick meal. He then changed his clothes and made his way directly to the procurator's palace. When he showed the regent's letter of recommendation, he was at once ushered into the presence of the overlord of Judea.

"You have a letter to deliver to me?" said the procurator. "Who are you, and what is your name?"

"I am a Judean, called Ithamar, my lord. I come from Rome. The noble tribune, Anejus Serranus, is my friend and protector." With these words he handed over the letter.

The procurator looked at it and examined the seal carefully. Then he removed the string and read in a loud voice:

To the honorable Pontius Pilatus, procurator of Judea, Lucius Aelius Sejanus, the emperor's deputy, sends greetings and wishes for prosperity.

The bearer of this letter, the Judean, Ithamar son of Elyakim, has been recommended to me by a good friend. Therefore I ask you to provide him with whatever protection or assistance he requires. Take care of your health. Yours affectionately,

Sejanus

"You are under my personal protection," said the procurator, when he had read the letter. "I shall give orders to admit you to my presence at all times, whether I am here or in Caesarea. Now tell me what I can do for you!"

"I thank you, my lord, for the assistance you have promised me. I shall turn to you whenever I need your help, but at present I have no special request to make. I have been away from Jerusalem for more than three years and must first determine the present position of my affairs. I have only just arrived, and since I was unaware of the contents of this letter, I considered it my first duty to fulfill my mission."

"Please return when you need me!"

Ithamar took his leave of the procurator and set out to find his father and Tirtzah. He saw many a familiar face in the streets of the city, but nobody recognized him, for a big black beard, which had grown during his absence from Jerusalem, had greatly altered his appearance.

Ithamar came to the house of Elazar ben Zevulun and entered. He knocked at the door of the sitting room and, on hearing a call to enter, did so. Elazar raised his eyes from the parchment roll in front of him and looked up at his visitor. Ithamar was shocked to see how withered the old man looked. He appeared listless and very depressed.

"Who are you?" the old man asked in a dull voice. "And what do you want from me? You are dressed like a Roman yet have the face of a Jew."

"I am a Jew," Ithamar replied, "but I come from Rome where I had to dress like a Roman, and I have not been in Jerusalem long enough to buy Jewish clothes. I came to you in order to find out how your friend Elyakim ben Chizkiyah is."

Elazar became more alert at the sound of the stranger's

voice. At his last words, he jumped up and exclaimed, "You are Ithamar! Blessed art Thou, Lord our God, King of the Universe, Who revivest the dead!"

With this, he hurried towards Ithamar, and sage and youth embraced, weeping loudly.

"Yes, I have been roused from the dead," said Ithamar. "Thanks to God's wonderful protection I have suffered three years of brutal slavery without coming to any physical or spiritual harm. Now, tell me, is my father still alive?"

When Elazar remained silent, a cry of pain burst from Ithamar's heart. He rent his garment, removed his shoes and spoke in heart-rending tones. "Blessed are Thou, Lord our God, King of the Universe, Thou faithful Judge." Thereupon, Ithamar let himself drop to the ground and cried softly to himself.

The sage looked on sadly as the youth mourned the death of his father. After a while he spoke, "You may rise now, Ithamar. The time of mourning was over long ago. It was only a few weeks after your arrest that he breathed his last. He was so depressed that he refused all comfort, and nobody was admitted to see him, not even I. However, when our honored prince, Rabban Gamliel, visited him, he had a long talk with him."

Ithamar had risen from the ground.

"One more question," he said. "How is your daughter Tirtzah? Is she still alive? Is she still unmarried?"

"She is alive and still unmarried."

"Blessed be the Lord, Who is kind and does kindness!"

"Do not rejoice too soon, Ithamar," said the sage, despondently. "Though Tirtzah is still unmarried, she is the bride of another man. The wedding is already arranged for next week."

"May that also be a blessing. It is sufficient that she is alive and well. Who is the happy man whom she has chosen?"

"She has not chosen anyone. She would have preferred to go to her grave mourning for you. However, she is forced to give her hand to Orev, your father's former slave."

The sage proceeded to tell the youth all that had happened.

XXI

THE REUNION

ITHAMAR LISTENED WITH great astonishment to the sage's story.

"Your father was actually the cause of our whole misfortune by appointing the slave as the heir to his property," Elazar concluded his account. "Though he could not foresee that you would ever come back healthy and free, nevertheless..."

"I beg you, Elazar, do not say anything against my dear, beloved and unforgettable father. Whatever he did was surely right and good," Ithamar interrupted him. "You told me that he spoke with the prince, Rabban Gamliel, a few weeks before his death. Surely he would not have acted without the agreement of the wisest man in Israel. I shall visit Rabban Gamliel; perhaps he has some news for me. Now tell me, where is Tirtzah?"

"She went out to visit a sick friend and is sure to be back soon. Stay here meanwhile and wait for her return. I cannot tell you how she wept and mourned your misfortune. And when we heard the news that the ship on which you were had been sunk..."

"Who invented that lie?"

"Orev told us about it."

"Orev and always Orev!" Ithamar shouted angrily. He was about to continue but restrained himself. When he remained silent, the sage continued, "You have not told me yet, Ithamar, how you escaped from slavery and regained your liberty."

Ithamar told him. He described the events in such a lively manner and Elazar listened so attentively, that neither of them noticed Tirtzah's entry into the room. Ithamar's back was turned to the door, so that Tirtzah could not see his face. But the voice—that she could not have forgotten. Suddenly Ithamar's account was interrupted by a cry, "Ithamar, you are alive!"

At once Ithamar turned round, for that voice went straight to his heart.

"Tirtzah!" he exclaimed.

Then Tirtzah said, "Blessed be the All Merciful God and blessed be His Name, since you are alive, healthy and free! Now I am willing to die."

"Why should you die, my Tirtzah? You shall live and be happy!"

"I am the bride of a man whom I despise."

"That bond will be severed."

"Did my father not tell you that he would then be condemned to shame and misery?"

"I shall speak to Rabban Gamliel. I have rich friends in Rome. Even the Roman procurator favors me. Ways and means will be found to set you free without exposing your father to misery."

"Do you really think so? If you could only achieve that I would gladly serve you as a maidservant all my life and fulfill the most lowly tasks."

"Not as my maidservant, but as my wife, as our fathers planned long ago."

"Look at me, Ithamar; grief and pain have long ago wiped out whatever beauty I may once have possessed."

" 'Grace is false and beauty is vain, a God-fearing wife is to be praised' [Proverbs, 31, 30]. I love you, Tirtzah, even if your beauty should have vanished forever. But you will blossom again like the roses of Jericho, once the worries are removed from your mind."

"What can release me from this hateful marriage?"

"I do not know as yet. But I am sure that the good Lord, Who has saved me in such a miraculous fashion, will not permit the raven (Orev) to devour my life's treasure. I do not possess the large sum of money which your father owes to my former slave, since I have been disinherited. Perhaps I can find friends who will lend it to me, and in case of need, the procurator will make sure that Orev extends the term when repayment is due."

"My dear Ithamar," said Elazar, "the sun is setting, and that is the time when Orev usually comes to visit us. I would not like you to meet him here."

"Nor would I," Ithamar replied. "I am leaving and shall come back tomorrow, God willing. I beg you not to tell my father's former steward of my return; otherwise he may take steps which might harm us. Tomorrow I shall visit him and see how he behaves towards me. Farewell, Elazar; farewell, my Tirtzah!"

"You must not call me that while I am still engaged to another man."

"I shall release you from that chain."

"God bless you, Ithamar, and lead you on the right path! But do take care that you do not draw misfortune upon your own head again!"

"You are so good, Tirtzah, and you worry more about me than about yourself. Have confidence in me; I shall keep my promise. I am firmly convinced that God, Who is most just, will see that justice is done to me."

"Farewell, my son," said Elazar. "May God in His holiness protect you."

Ithamar went to the house of the prince. However, He could not speak to him at once since Rabban Gamliel had gone to visit the procurator. The prince's servants told him that he was only expected home late that night and would then soon retire to bed, for he was weak. Ithamar returned to his inn. He ordered food and drink to be brought to his room but could only eat very little. He prayed the evening prayers and retired to bed, but sleep escaped him. The news he had been told that day had greatly excited him. Why had his father appointed the slave as his heir, his father who had loved his only son so much? Why had he not entrusted his property to the care of the law-courts, in case his son returned? If Elyakim had considered that impossible, why did he not bequeath his wealth to charitable institutions? Why had he appointed the slave, whom he had refused to set free during his lifetime, as master? Could the will be a forgery? In that case, why did the authorities not dispute it?

Midnight was long past and dawn was rising in the east when Ithamar fell into a restless sleep. In his dreams his father appeared to him and said, "Go to Rabban Gamliel; he will answer all your questions!"

When Ithamar woke from his sleep, it was already broad daylight. He rose, washed his hands and face, dressed, took out *talith* and *tefillin* and went to the synagogue which was in Rabban Gamliel's house. The prince was already there. After the morning service, Ithamar approached the prince, who stretched out his hand to him and said, "Peace be with you, son of Elyakim!"

"Peace be with you, my master and my teacher. My prince has recognized me?"

"Yesterday the procurator informed me of your return. Praised be the Lord, Who releaseth the bound. Follow me to my room. I have important information for you."

XXII

THE MEETING

ITHAMAR WAS RADIANT WITH joy when he left Rabban Gamliel's house. The prince had invited him for breakfast and after the meal had given him news which filled the young man's heart with great satisfaction. As he was on his way to visit his father's house, a man hastened towards him, calling out from the distance, "Blessed be He Who reviveth the dead. Peace be with you, my dear, beloved friend."

Ithamar recognized the voice that called to him. He ran to meet his approaching friend, embraced him and said, "Elazar, my brother, blessed be the Lord Who has kept you alive. How is your father? How are all our friends?"

"My father is no longer with us. God has taken him away. Now he is next to the divine throne, together with the other great men of our people. At his funeral, an impressive looking sage, whom nobody knew, joined in the procession. People claimed that he was the prophet Yechezkel, who wanted to honor my dear father, peace be upon him, because he had saved the Book of

Yechezkel. As to our friends, they are all well and sound. Ithamar, Ithamar, how much grief and pain you have caused us. If you had only told me that day in the cave that you had entrusted our secret to that disgraceful slave, then all our misfortunes might have been prevented."

"Then you know about him, my friend?"

"I saw through your Orev long ago. Rabban Gamliel also saw through him, and accordingly he advised your father, of blessed memory, how to make his arrangements."

"So you know that as well?"

"That, too, was not difficult to understand. The whole city was indignant about your father's will, but I listened to the adverse comments of the people and remained silent. Why should I speak when Rabban Gamliel remained silent! Where are you going now?"

"I want to visit the slave and call him to account."

"Let me come with you, and if you do not mind, let us first go to see our friend Barak and ask him to accompany us."

"Are you afraid for my sake? Do not worry, Elazar; my father's old servants would not permit even one hair of mine to be harmed."

"You do not seem to know that Orev has dismissed all your father's Jewish servants and sold all his slaves. He has surrounded himself with a new staff."

"And did that not arouse public opinion against him?"

"Not at all. They thought his behavior was clever and

right. Since he had now become the master, he required the respect of his servants and slaves. Now you see that there is nobody in your father's house who would take your part if Orev had evil designs against you."

Elazar took Ithamar's arm and led him through various streets till they reached the house of their mutual friend, Barak.

"Look, my friend, whom I bring you here!" called Elazar to the master of the house.

Barak stood up, shook hands with Elazar and looked at Ithamar.

"Welcome, stranger," he said. "You must be a good man since Elazar is introducing you to me. But I do not remember having seen your face before."

"It is Ithamar ben Elyakim, from the house of Nachshon!"

Barak embraced his former companion with great joy.

"Blessed be the Lord Who reviveth the dead," he said. "You have truly returned from the dead. Sit down, my friend, and tell me in what miraculous manner God has saved you and brought you back to us."

"We have not got time for that now," Elazar said. "Our friend will tell you everything in detail later. Now, above all else, he must try to win back his paternal inheritance."

"You unfortunate lad," said Barak, "you have been disinherited. I was so upset by your father's strange will!"

"I beg you not to judge rashly, Barak," replied Ithamar. "The greatest wisdom..."

"Let us not waste time discussing matters," Elazar interjected. "It is essential that we go to see Orev immeiately before rumors of your return spread through the city and reach the ears of that disgraceful slave, for then he might take steps to harm us."

"I do not understand a single word of all this," said Barak.

"Be patient, my Barak," Elazar replied. "You will hear everything and learn to understand. But now, do us the favor of accompanying us to the house of Ithamar's father. When Orev sees that Ithamar's friends stand by him, he will not dare to take any violent measures against him."

Barak declared himself ready to come, and the three young men set out on their way. When Ithamar crossed the threshold of his father's house, he was overcome by his emotions. He stopped, and tears flowed from his eyes.

"Be a man, Ithamar," Elazar warned him. "This is not the time to cry but to fight."

A slave approached and asked what they wanted.

"Tell your master that I, Elazar ben Chananyah ben Chizkiyah ben Gorion, and two of my friends wish to speak to him."

"Sorry sir," replied the slave, "but I cannot remember all those names."

"Then simply say ben Gorion!"

A few minutes later Orev hurried towards them.

"What a joy for my house!" he cried. "The noblest man in Judea, the famous and celebrated Elazar, honors me with a visit. Heartfelt welcome to you. And you, honorable gentlemen, since you are friends of the noble Elazar, you are just as welcome here. I have the pleasure of knowing you, noble Barak. But who are you, stranger, dressed like a Roman? The stamp of the divine likeness in your refined features suggests that you are a son of Judah."

"Orev," said Ithamar, "look at me more closely!"

The sound of this voice burst on Orev like a thunder-clap; he turned pale and his knees shook. "Ithamar," he mumbled in consternation. But then he pulled himself together, and stretched out his arms and cried, "Come to my heart, you precious son of my beloved master!"

Ithamar, too, controlled himself and accepted Orev's embrace, though without any enthusiasm.

"This is indeed a happy day," the former slave cried out, "since you, my dear Ithamar, are still alive and well, and God has brought you back to your home. God has sanctified this day, let us be happy and rejoice on it! I shall at once order a festive meal to be prepared in honor of the safe return of my dear Ithamar. You, honored gentlemen, shall stay with me. Perseus, run along and invite the sages of Israel to a banquet. Ask the prince, Rabban Gamliel, and his son Shimon, the wise Yochanan ben Zakkai, as well as my future father-in-law, Elazar ben Zevulun of the house of Azaryah and all the others! Anchises," he called to another slave, "give orders for a big feast to be prepared. Let them take the best food from the larder and cellar, in order to entertain our guests in a fitting manner. Now, gentlemen, come into my private study, and you, Ithamar, must tell me all the wonderful events that happened to you, so that I too may praise God for all the miracles which He performed for you in such abundant measure!"

The young men followed the master of the house into his room. He asked them to be seated, and slaves offered them wine and cake.

"There you are," Orev said. "Take some refreshments, and then Ithamar must tell me his story. I long to hear how you escaped from brutal slavery."

XXIII

THE SLAVE IS EXPOSED

"EXCUSE ME, OREV," ELAZAR said, "but before drinking your wine and eating your food, I . . ."

"You can be perfectly at ease, noble Elazar," Orev interrupted him. "In my house everything is observed exactly as in my dear master Elyakim's lifetime. All food and drink is prepared with the same care for purity and sanctity as in his lifetime."

"But what about the foreign slaves you have taken into your household?"

"I have had them trained carefully, and I myself supervise them strictly. How else would I dare to invite Rabban Gamliel and the sages into my house for a meal?"

Then the young men accepted a little food and wine, and Ithamar began to speak, "I have not much to tell you. You will probably remember, Orev, that Roman, Serranus, whom we together saved and sustained in Jaffa when his ship had sunk and he was washed ashore by the waves and lay there unconscious. The emperor appointed him admiral of the fleet which has just defeated the pirates. He recognized me and took me to Rome with him, and there he obtained my release. The emperor's deputy, mighty Sejanus, gave me a letter of recommendation to Pontius Pilatus, the procurator of Judea, which I have already delivered to him yesterday. He received me in a very friendly manner and assured me of his protection and his help in case of need."

When Orev heard these words he grew pale. He had made generous presents to the procurator in order to be sure of his favor and to be able to make use of his protection in case Ithamar returned and contested Elyakim's will. Now he had to abandon that hope. But he forced a smile to his face. "Why should you need the help and protection of the procurator?"

"I do not know either," replied Ithamar. "Now, Orev, tell me about my father's last days and about his arrangements for the distribution of his fortune."

"Your father was extremely depressed by the misfortune which had befallen you and survived for only a few weeks. Your friends will have told you that he appointed me his heir, since he had given up any hope of your return. His will was drawn up by the sages of Israel and confirmed by the Roman authorities. I shall hand you a copy of it during the coming banquet, in the presence of the sages of Israel. You will then be able to convince yourself that the document is perfectly genuine and legal. It would be futile to try and contest it."

"I would not dream of it. My father's last will is sacred to me and I consider it incontestable."

Orev would have like to dance with joy when he heard these words, but he controlled himself and said, "You are a good and noble son! I am very sorry that you have to go away empty-handed. I would gladly share my inheritance with you. But I have taken on additional obligations since, which make that impossible. Tirtzah, the daughter of Elazar ben Zevulun of the house of Azaryah, has agreed to become my wife, and I have promised her father to make her the mistress of my entire fortune."

"Then you have taken my place in that respect as well, and intend to marry the bride who was destined for me? I beg you, Orev, stand back and leave my bride to me."

"Forgive me, Ithamar, if I do not comply with your wishes in this respect. I also have loved Tirtzah for a long time, and life has no value for me if I have to relinquish possession of her. If you love the girl truly, you must admit that I am able to offer my wife a better life than you are."

"You are right. I am poor and possess only the remainder of the sum of money which Serranus was kind enough to present to me, whereas you are wealthy and in full possession of all the property which my father bequeathed to you."

"I feel sorry for you, Ithamar. But you must not ask me to give up the happiness of my life. Tirtzah, too, is poor, for her father owns next to nothing, as his debts exceed the value of his property. Perhaps I can be of use to you in some other way?"

"Perhaps you might give me the job of managing one

of the estates which once belonged to my father."

"Surely you are not serious about that. It would be unseemly for you to be employed by me. That would arouse everybody's indignation and would always give you cause for dissatisfaction. You must find another way of earning a living. Rent a small property in one of the villages and work on it. If you should ever be in need, you can count on me to support you willingly."

At these words of Orev, Barak jumped up. He seemed prepared to knock the master of the house to the ground. Elazar forced him to sit down again.

"I beg of you," he whispered, "remain calm and wait patiently till we see what happens."

"No, I do not think that is likely," said Ithamar. "My friend and patron Serranus has offered to give me one of his Spanish estates. If I cannot earn a livelihood at home, I shall accept his offer and move across the seas. There is already a large Jewish settlement in that distant land, and I shall be able to live in the community of Toledo according to our Law."

"I am delighted to hear that you have such good prospects. You should not hesitate to accept the generous gift of the noble Roman."

"For the time being I prefer to remain in the land of my fathers. God will help me to earn a living so that I need not accept charity of other men."

"You are still the proud, noble youth that you used to be. But believe me, although you have refused my offer, I shall not refrain from repeating it, if you should need it."

"I admire your generosity, Orev," Elazar said smiling.

"Till now I had imagined that former slaves did not share that inherited virtue of Israel—charitableness."

Orev ground his teeth. He would have liked to strangle the man, but he suppressed his anger and said, "I try to follow my dear master, Elyakim, in all things. Just as he was always charitable, I am too. The poor of Jerusalem can confirm that."

"Certainly, my dear Orev," Elazar said with a wry smile. "They talk about it everywhere when you have been charitable to the poor. And how you honor your dead master and patron we have just seen in the alacrity and the kind manner with which you welcomed the son of your former master. I am firmly convinced that you will reap a reward for your noble deeds, and our eyes will see with great joy how rich that reward will be."

XXIV

THE DESTRUCTION OF WICKEDNESS

THE LARGE HALL HAD TABLES richly set for the guests. Gold and silver vessels were laid out in abundance. These were precious not only because of the great value of the metals, but even more so on account of the great artistry with which they had been fashioned. Here you could see goblets and bowls of pure gold, shaped by the artistic hands of Greek goldsmiths into real works of art. Here also were tablemats and basins of precious silver, craftsmen's work, so lovely and beautiful that the eyes of an observer could only rest on them in admiring fascination. Rare flowers decorated the table and spread a pleasant perfume. Censers containing Indian incense hung suspended in the corners of the hall. These would be lit in the course of the meal, in order to refresh the guests with their precious and unusual scent. And what a gathering of noble guests were assembled here! Above all, Rabban Gamliel, the universally admired prince, together with his son Shimon, who was already acknowledged as a great teacher in Israel; Yochanan ben Zakkai, the youngest, but not the least, pupil of the unforgettable Hillel; Azaryah, a priest of the generation of Ezra, the father of Rabbi Elazar ben Azaryah, who was later to become very famous; Yossi ben Hyrkanos, Nachum from Gamzu, and many, many others. Servants moved about with silver jugs and basins, while others handed out towels. The guests washed their hands and sat down to their appointed places. Rabban Gamliel broke the bread and said the blessing in a loud voice: "Blessed art Thou, Lord our God, King of the Universe, Who brings forth bread from the earth." A loud "Amen" rang forth and the meal began. Servants hastened to fill the goblets with delicious wine, stronger in flavor than the perfume of flowers.

Orev rose and said, "Welcome, my exalted teachers and honored guests! This is the first time that I have had the pleasure of entertaining you in my house. I dare not ascribe this great honor to myself, but rather to the presence of my dear guest, Ithamar ben Elyakim. He has returned to us, contrary to all expectations, and I would now therefore like to fulfill in your presence—before we enjoy the pleasures of the feast—the provisions laid down by Elyakim's will in case of his son's return. I have here a copy of this testament which was deposited with the Roman authorities. Permit me to read it out loud, honored prince of Israel."

Rabban Gamliel nodded in agreement, and Orev read, "With the help of God, I, the undersigned Elyakim, son of Chizkiyah, of the house of Nachshon, bequeath all my property to my present steward, Orev, as his complete and exclusive property and possession. In case my son, Ithamar, should at any time return to Jerusalem, he may demand any one item of my heritage, according to his own choice, and Orev will be obliged to hand over the article of his choice, whatsoever that may be, without any refusal or argument, into Ithamar's possession. This is my last will, which I confirm and attest by my signature and that of suitable witnesses."

"This testament has been signed by Elyakim and by the witnesses," continued Orev. "Both the Jewish and the Roman authorities have confirmed it. Therefore, I took over possession of Elyakim's property some years ago, and I am ready now to fulfill the provision laid down for the unexpected return of Ithamar. Choose any item, my Ithamar, according to your own free will. Look at this enormous golden goblet; it is a unique work of art and extremely valuable. I would advise you to choose that, but if you desire something else, look around you; there are sufficient treasures spread out before your eyes. Let the most noble and distinguished men of Judea act as witnesses that I have not limited your choice in any way."

Orev sat down and Ithamar rose to reply.

"I thank you for your good advice, Orev, but I do not intend to choose this goblet. I want to choose something still more valuable and precious. You see, Orev, you have taken my place entirely. You are the owner of all the treasures collected by my ancestors, you are the owner of all the estates inherited or acquired by my ancestors, and you are the fiancé of the girl who was destined for me.

How highly my father must have valued and esteemed you that he appointed you heir to his princely fortune! How highly Tirtzah, the daughter of Elazar of the royal house of Azaryah, must have esteemed you that she agreed to become your wife! Therefore, without any doubt, you are the most precious and valuable item in the entire inheritance of my father, and therefore I choose you! You shall become my property, my slave, just as you were my father's slave!"

"Have you gone mad?" cried Orev.

"No, he is not mad, but on the contrary, he has made the right choice as intended by his father," said Rabban Gamliel. "You have never received a letter of release, Orev, though you would indeed have become free if Ithamar had not returned. Now, however, he has inherited you and taken possession of you, according to his father's will. Together with you, all that you have considered as your property up till now rightly belongs to him, since a slave's property belongs to his master."

"Ha, ha," cried Orev, "we are under Roman rule, and the procurator, whose favor I enjoy, will not permit such injustice to be done to me. I shall fight for my rights, even if I have to donate half my property to the Romans."

"You are mistaken, Orev," said Rabban Gamliel. "I visited the procurator yesterday. He told me that Ithamar had returned and brought him a letter of recommendation from mighty Sejanus, the emperor's deputy. I explained the position to the procurator immediately, for you ought to know that Elyakim worded his will in this way on my advice. Our aim was to avoid confiscation of his property after his death, since without such a will, it would have belonged to Ithamar whom the Romans had condemned. By making this will, however, it would be preserved for the son, in case of his return. Pontius Pilatus accepted my exposition and has confirmed it in writing through his secretary, as you see here. Therefore, you cannot expect any assistance from the Romans. You must accept the inevitable. After all, you are only returning to your former state."

"Orev," Ithamar said, "I could forgive you your cold manner towards me this morning; I could forgive you for forcing Tirtzah to become engaged to you, whom she hates and despises. But tell me, how can I forgive how you betrayed me three years ago, how you betrayed my father's absolute trust in you and stole his money in order to ensure my condemnation? Thus you brought my father's gray head in grief to his grave. How can I forget the three terrible years which I spent in brutal slavery? Thanks to you, I was forced to eat forbidden food and to work on the Sabbath and I was prevented from fulfilling God's holy commandments!"

"Curse you," Orev shouted and ran from the hall. Elazar ben Chananyah tried to hold him back, but Ithamar called to him, "Let him go, Elazar!"

Orev went to his room with desperation in his heart. No one else had ever been cast from the pinnacle of happiness into the deepest night of misery. For a moment, he thought of escaping with as much of his treasures as possible, but he soon gave up the idea as impracticable.

Meanwhile, the friends surrounded the reinstated son and congratulated him. But Ithamar released himself from them and hastened to Rabban Gamliel. He seized the prince's hand and brought it to his lips.

"My prince, my teacher, my father," he cried, "how can I thank you!"

"You owe me no thanks," said the prince. "I did no more than my duty, which I would have done for the least worthy man in Israel, how much more so for the son of my friend and fellow student, with whom I sat together at the feet of my unforgettable grandfather and teacher, Hillel."

Ithamar looked around for Elazar ben Zevulun. He wished to embrace the father of his Tirtzah, but Elazar had already hastened home, in order to inform his daughter of the good news.

A slave entered the hall and announced sadly, "My master, Orev..."

"Your fellow slave Orev," Ithamar thundered.

"My fellow slave Orev..." the slave mumbled, unable to continue.

"Well," Ithamar asked, "what about him?"

"He has hanged himself."

XXV

ACROSS THE SEAS

THE SLAVE HAD HARDLY FINished speaking when Elazar ben Chananyah ben Chizkiyah ben Gorion left the house in haste. He was soon followed by those guests who were, like himself, descendants of the priestly tribe, since the house was made impure through the presence of the corpse. All the learned men who had been guests in the house had to purify themselves. On the third and seventh day of their purification, they had to be sprinkled with the water of purification, which had been mixed with the ashes of the red cow, and on the seventh day they had to immerse themselves in the ritual bath. Only on that evening did they become pure again. Elazar ben Zevulun had avoided all this, for he had left the house while Orev was still in the dining hall. Though not of priestly descent, he practiced the priestly rules of purity like all the *chaverim* (companions, as the scholars called themselves) of his time. Since Tirtzah attended to her father's domestic requirements, she was also unable to meet Ithamar during that period. The day after his purification,

Ithamar offered a great sacrifice of thanksgiving and joy. On the same day, he renewed his engagement to his beloved, and a few weeks later they celebrated their wedding with rejoicing and jubilation.

Elazar ben Zevulun still lived to see his daughter present him with a grandson, whom he could swing on his knees. A few years later he laid down his weary head to rest and was gathered to his fathers. He died peacefully, since he knew that his only daughter was protected by the man for whom she had been destined from early childhood.

For the Jewish people, too, a peaceful period appeared to dawn. After the fall of the emperor's favorite, Sejanus, Vitellius was appointed governor of Syria. Vitellius, who was a friend of the Jews, kept Pontius Pilatus, the procurator of Judea, in check, and when complaints were nevertheless raised against him, he deposed him and sent him back to Rome. But even better things were in store for Judea. Agrippas—a grandson of Herod the Great and his wife, the Hasmonean princess Mariamne—had spent his youth in Rome and been a friend of the heir apparent, Orusus. When Sejanus had had this prince removed from his path by means of poison, Agrippas had to escape from Rome. After an adventurous life, spent in poverty and squalor, he returned to Rome after the fall of Sejanus, and there he soon became one of the most intimate friends of Caius Caligula, the heir to the throne. One day, he expressed the wish that the Emperor Tiberius should die soon, so that a more worthy man, Caligula, might ascend the throne. This opinion was reported to the old emperor, and Agrippas was cast in prison where he had to suffer for six months, shackled by iron chains. Then the Emperor Tiberius was murdered, and the new emperor, Caligula, hastened to free his friend from prison. In the place of iron chains which he had been forced to wear, he presented him with a golden chain. He set a diadem upon his head and appointed him king of Judea.

Agrippas made great efforts to do his best for his fellow Jews, as far as it lay in his power. However, he was king in name only, and the Romans continued to be the real rulers of Judea.

The Emperor Caligula, who in his youth had shown promise of becoming a good ruler, later went mad and hated the Jews because they refused to acknowledge and honor him as a god. He ordered his statue to be set up in the Holy Temple in Jerusalem and that it should be accorded divine honor. Petronius, the governor of Syria, received instructions to enforce the emperor's wish by force of arms. A terrible fear gripped the whole Jewish nation, and all were prepared to die rather than tolerate the desecration of the Holy House of God. Elazar ben Chananyah ben Chizkiyah called his friends together to consider the best way of meeting force with force. Ithamar, too, was invited to the meeting, and when he did not appear, Elazar ben Chananyah went to see him personally, in order to induce him to take part in the organization of the revolt.

"My heart bleeds at the thought that I cannot fight at your side," said Ithamar, "but I am bound by my oath."

"That oath is no longer valid," replied Elazar. "They want to set up an idol in the Holy Temple and you talk about your oath! Surely we are bound by the prior oath which we swore at Mount Sinai not to allow idolatry?"

"You are right there," Ithamar said, "but let us wait a little longer and see what happens."

Ithamar remembered the regrets he had had for his rash behavior on that other occasion and how he had decided never to join in the activities of young men without the consent of the great sages of Israel.

"Perhaps Agrippas or one of the diplomats will be able to achieve the annulment of this evil decree," continued Ithamar.

"Even if that comes to pass, we cannot be sure that no similar evil decree will ever again be issued by the emperor or his successor. Now is the time to act and to rebel against the wicked government."

"But my oath forbids me to rebel!"

"Years of slavery have broken your spirit and do not allow you to see the matter from the correct viewpoint."

"Elazar!" The latter turned his face away and left the house in anger. Ithamar remained alone, his heart full of distress.

"I cannot bear it," he said to his wife, Tirtzah, who had entered the room. "I feel despised and humiliated before my friends."

"Did you not tell me that the powerful Roman Serranus has promised to give you an estate in Spain? Let us move there. Then you will be free from the temptation to rebel."

"But how can I leave my people at a time of danger? How can I forsake our holy land?"

On this occasion, the danger did pass, just as Ithamar had hoped. Agrippas succeeded in persuading the emperor to annul the decree. He arranged a great banquet in honor of the emperor and his favorites, and when Caligula had drunk to his heart's content, he suggested that Agrippas should ask him a favor—and Agrippas begged him to annul the decree. But it did not take long till things turned out as Elazar had foreseen. A few months later, the emperor issued a new order to set up his statue in the Temple. This time, no one was able to effect an annulment. Even the efforts of Philo of Alexandria, the influential philosopher, were without any success. But the Holy One, Blessed be He, heard the prayers of His people and performed a miracle for them. The Emperor Caligula was murdered by conspirators. King Agrippas made great efforts to ensure the election of Claudius as Roman Emperor. When his efforts bore fruit and the Senate confirmed the election, Claudius recognized Agrippas' activities on his behalf and showed him kindness. Now Judea could again enjoy a period of peace and quiet. When, shortly after this, Agrippas fell ill and died, Judea became again entirely dependent on the whims and desires of the Roman rulers.

During the reign of Agrippas, Ithamar finally gave in to his wife's pleadings, for it was obvious that the destruction of the Temple was approaching, and every man who gave the matter any thought had to realize that the prophecy of Daniel would soon be fulfilled. Thus, after having sold all his property, Ithamar and his family moved to Spain. In this way, he was at least spared the pain of witnessing the events which took place in Judea at the time of the destruction of our Holy Temple. The majority of Jews in Jerusalem did not survive that period, and those who did survive would have preferred death to such a life. In this way, too, Ithamar escaped the temptation of participating in the rebellion against the Roman government.

From afar, Ithamar mourned bitterly the loss of Israel's glory. He spent the greater part of his fortune in redeeming the Jewish captives whom the wicked Titus had sent to Spain, and he did his best to alleviate their suffering and to set up a home for them in the distant west until the Lord would again show mercy to His people and send them the Redeemer—may it be soon, in our days.

A man traveled across the ocean and left one son who sat and studied Torah in the land of Israel. When the time came for him to die, he bequeathed all his property to his slave and wrote to his son that he should choose one item for himself out of all the property which he had bequeathed to the slave. When the master died, the slave collected together the whole fortune and took it along with him, together with the testament, till he arrived in the land of Israel. Then he said to the son, "Your father has died and bequeathed all his possessions to me except for any one item which you may choose for yourself." What did the son do? He went to his teacher and told him the whole story. His teacher said to him, "Your father was a very wise man and learned in legal matters. He must have thought to himself, 'If I leave my possessions in charge of my slave, he will steal or lose them. Instead, I will give them to him as a gift, whereupon he will take good care of them. My son will have the opportunity to choose one item for himself, and if he chooses the slave, the property will all revert to him!' "

This he did, and the court gave him both the property and the slave, for when a slave acquires property, he and his property belong to his master.

King Shlomo said, "[God] has given wisdom and knowledge to the man who appears good before Him": this applies to the father. "But to the sinner, He gave an interest in amassing and preserving property": this refers to the slave. "In order to give it to him who appears good before the Lord": this applies to the son, for the Holy One, Blessed be He, keeps the property of the wicked for the righteous."

Midrash Tanchuma, Lech Lecha, 8

Marcus Lehmann

THE AGUNAH

Translated from the German

FELDHEIM PUBLISHERS Ltd.
Jerusalem ✤ New York

Originally published in German
under the title Die Verlassene

First published in English, 1981
ISBN 0-87306-282-5

Phototypeset at the Feldheim Press

Philipp Feldheim Inc.
96 East Broadway
New York, NY 10002

Feldheim Publishers Ltd
POB 6525 / Jerusalem, Israel

Printed in Israel

I

THE WEDDING

THE AFTERNOON SUN WAS shining, but inside the synagogue of P., the glow of the flickering gas lights added to the atmosphere of expectancy. They illuminated the flower-bedecked galleries and the richly carpeted floor. Carriages were drawn up in front of the building, their coachmen and attendants wearing flowers in their buttonholes.

The well trained choir in the synagogue was accompanied by a powerful organ. A wedding ceremony was about to be performed, and the rabbi was waiting in front of the Ark. The synagogue was packed to capacity when the doors opened and a procession entered. Black-robed beadles appeared with their white silk *taleisim* draped over their shoulders and torches in their hands. They moved forward with great dignity and were followed by the bridegroom, accompanied by his family. All eyes were on the bridegroom.

"What a handsome man," a young lady whispered to her older neighbor.

"*Mais il a trop vegu!* But he has lived a gay life!" the

latter responded, and the pale, indolent, though intelligent face of the bridegroom seemed to confirm her view.

When the bridegroom had assumed his position under the bridal canopy, facing the rabbi, the doors of the synagogue were flung open once again. The torch bearers reappeared, followed by the bride who was surrounded by many young ladies dressed in white.

"Has the bride no mother?" the lady who had previously admired the bridegroom addressed her neighbor.

"She has both a father and a mother, but they were opposed to her marriage to Dr. Zevulun, and therefore they would not attend the wedding. Her parents are strictly Orthodox and would not even enter a Reform synagogue. The bridegroom is known as a loose fellow, and the parents were strongly opposed to the match. Still, their only daughter has achieved her aim. But hush, quiet now. The organ has stopped and the preacher is about to begin his address!"

The preacher spoke. Have you ever heard the sermon of a Reform rabbi, dear reader? He pours out words of honey which have been carefully planned to suit the taste of his hearers. There is no word of admonition or criticism, not the slightest hint of any unpleasantness, no mention of divine commandments, but only flattery, designed to please everybody.

The preacher praised the bridegroom's intellect and his holy profession as a medical man. He praised the bride's will-power in cutting herself loose from restrictive and oppressive prejudices, in spite of numerous obstacles. He spoke of the admiration which the unbaised

Jew aroused in the minds of intelligent non-Jews and of the wife's duty to raise herself to the spiritual level of her husband. Then he laid his hands on the heads of the bridal pair and blessed them. The bridegroom put the wedding ring on the bride's finger and spoke the decisive words.

Now she was his wife, tied to the man of her choice with strong bonds which only death or divorce could sever. Who could have imagined in this hour of happiness and joy, that this bride, Fredericka Salz, would one day wait with longing for definite news of her husband's death or for his letter of divorce?

Fredericka Salz was the only daughter of a wealthy wholesale merchant, Mr. Simon Salz of P. Mr. and Mrs. Salz had been married for twenty years when the wife gave birth to this daughter, long after they had given up any hope of ever having children of their own. The parents' happiness was so overwhelming, their love for the child of their old age so tender, that they spoiled their daughter completely. Even her most absurd demands were promptly carried out, so that she became extremely self-centered. Since the little girl was fond of learning, she received a good education, which, however, unfortunately failed to correct the faults of her character. When Fredericka reached the age of fifteen, she had grown into a beautiful and intelligent girl. It was then that young Dr. Zevulun returned from university and settled down as a doctor in his hometown, P. Soon, all Fredericka's friends were talking about the clever and handsome doctor. Fredericka met him at the house of her friends. The young man paid more attention to her than to the others, and this flattered Fredericka. The two met frequently, and one day, Dr. Zevulun visited the wealthy merchant and asked for the hand of his only daughter. Old Mr. Salz was taken aback by what he considered impudence.

"But Dr. Zevulun," he said, "when we met in the street a few weeks ago on the Sabbath, you were smoking a cigar in public! How could you marry my daughter?"

"I must admit that I have not paid attention to Jewish ceremonial till now. But if you like..."

"If I like? It would indeed be a strange kind of piety if it appeared only in response to my wishes. No, my dear sir, it is quite impossible."

"I would like to point out to you, Mr. Salz, that your daughter loves me and that I speak to you with her consent."

"Is that true? That would be a great misfortune."

"Sir, you insult me!"

"Please keep calm, Dr. Zevulun. After all, we know each other. We both know how you behaved while you were studying in Vienna."

Dr. Zevulun was too disconcerted to reply.

"Now that we have finished our conversation," said Mr. Salz, "I would like to be left alone, for I am very busy."

"Are you showing me the door, Mr. Salz? Do you realize that the happiness of your only daughter is at stake?"

"It is for that very reason that I can never approve of her marriage to you."

"But, Mr. Salz, I promise you that I will change my way of life completely."

"Then you must first demonstrate this change by your actions. That would be to your advantage as well."

"Would you agree to our betrothal if I give you no cause for complaint during the next year?"

"I would still refuse to give you my daughter. The change must come from your own heart. An improvement merely for the sake of certain worldly considerations is of no permanent value."

Dr. Zevulun left in a rage. He was not alone in his anger. Fredericka too was annoyed with her father and called him a tyrant. For the first time in her life he had refused to comply with her wishes. She wept, stormed, demanded, implored, and when she saw that it was all in vain, she fell ill. Fredericka was not pretending, for that was not her nature. Impotent rage had really made her seriously ill. Her mother sat by her bedside and wept day and night, while her old father shed bitter tears. Their famous family doctor declared that he was unable to help them. Reluctantly, Mr. Salz decided to call Dr. Zevulun. When he appeared, Fredericka improved almost immediately. Mrs. Salz now implored her husband not to endanger their daughter's life again.

Mr. Salz called his daughter to his room. There he told her, with affection and kindness, all the derogatory tales he had heard about Dr. Zevulun. But Fredericka remained adamant.

"Well then, you may marry him," said Mr. Salz eventually. "I shall not curse you, and I will provide you with a considerable dowry. But on the day that you become Mrs. Zevulun you will no longer be my child. Neither I nor your mother will take part in your wedding celebrations. You must choose between us and him."

As we have seen, Fredericka made her choice. But Mr. Salz too kept his word. While hundreds of happy guests celebrated the wedding, the bride's parents did not share in their joy. The wedding guests danced till the early hours of the morning while Mr. and Mrs. Salz sat alone at home and wept. Their house was as lonely as it had been before the birth of their daughter. But now the situation was even worse. Before, their contentment had been disturbed by unsatisfied longing, whereas now, their longing had been fulfilled, but their heartache had increased.

How can any man know what is best for him! It is for this reason that a Jew wishes his friend, "May God fulfill your heart's desire in such a way that it will be for your good!"

II

STRANGE DISAPPEARANCE

FREDERICKA'S WEDDING HAD taken place in late autumn. The following summer, the young couple planned to go away for their honeymoon. In vain did Dr. and Mrs. Zevulun try to approach her parents. Mr. Salz remained firm, and his wife obeyed his wishes. Meanwhile, Fredericka had no cause for complaint against her husband, who was always loving and considerate to her. He allowed her to run the household according to Jewish law and to observe the Jewish marital laws. Fredericka's dowry had been invested in safe shares, and Dr. Zevulun's income from the practice was ample for the needs of the household, as he was both skillful and popular.

Till August, Dr. Zevulun could not leave his patients, but then he was able to arrange for some colleagues to take his place while he was away. Thus, he was free to travel to Vienna with his young wife to see the celebrations held to mark the emperor's return from Hungary. This was the year 1852, a few years after the Hungarian revolution of 1848. The revolt had been suppressed with Russia's aid. The great Hungarian generals who had been defeated had either been taken prisoner or had left the country together with Kossuth and other insurrectionist leaders. Now Hungary was as quiet as the grave. The emperor had just visited this imperial realm and had been well received everywhere. One could assume that Hungary was again genuinely Austrian, its liberties and privileges forgotten, and reunited with the House of Habsburg through the emperor's great kindness. In the other parts of Austria, too, the constitution of 1848 had been annulled and absolute rule reestablished. To mark the occasion, orders had gone out for a festive reception of the emperor in Vienna, and the Viennese people complied with their customary alacrity. Elaborate preparations were made, and thousands of strangers poured into Vienna in order to participate in the celebrations. Among these visitors were Dr. Zevulun and his wife.

Fredericka had never been to Vienna before. In order to enjoy the attractions of the capital at their leisure the young couple arrived there on Sunday, though the celebrations were only due to begin on the following Saturday, continuing for a whole week.

A happy time now ensued for the young wife. Her husband, usually so busy, now belonged to her alone. Arm in arm they wandered through the city of Vienna while he showed her the art treasures and unusual sights and, with his wide knowledge, explained everything to her. They spent long hours in the art gallery at Belvedere. In the afternoons, they went on excursions to Nussdorf or Baden, to the Kahlenberg or to Hietzing. Evenings were spent in the theater where they were amused by comedians or saw the actors of the Bingtheater in classical plays. Once, they listened to the wonderful orchestra in the Karnthmertor. Friday night brought its own special pleasure. The singing of Cantor Sulzer and his choir delighted Fredericka, but she felt embarrassed when she realized that, as the ladies' gallery was unenclosed, she was attracting people's attention and that more than one lorgnette was turned deliberately towards her. When she complained about this at supper in the Jewish restaurant, one of her husband's acquaintances jokingly replied, "It's quite all right, Mrs. Zevulun. Our Rabbi Mannheimer preached two sermons to us on the last two Saturdays. The first one he called 'Looking up,' the second 'Looking down.' So that is how we have divided things up. We men have taken to 'looking up,' while the ladies do the 'looking down.' "

This frivolous joke was well received and caused much laughter. Nevertheless, Fredericka felt that she could pray more devoutly in the Orthodox synagogue at home, without the distraction of curious stares.

On Saturday afternoon at three o'clock, the capital, adorned with flowers, flags and carpets, welcomed its beloved monarch! He arrived at the railway station, surrounded by Hungarian nobles in their national costume. The emperor's mother, all the Austrian nobility and the city fathers were there to receive him. The mayor of Vienna made an impressive speech. Then the splendid company moved through the streets, and from every window, sightseers who had paid a high price for the privilege, looked down on the sight. The Jews too had sent their rabbi, with a Torah scroll, to welcome the emperor. A large crowd of Jews surrounded him, and the police were called out to ensure order.

In the written accounts of the festivities, this Jewish share in the celebrations was duly mentioned and praised, but the latent anti-Semitism, too, did not fail to peep through. The report stressed that the police had to be brought in especially to supervise the unruly Jewish crowd.

There were grand illuminations in the evening, and the streets were flooded with lights. The high dome of St. Stephen's Cathedral was lit from below by spotlights. Artistic posters of various kinds adorned many buildings. The city's synagogue too was decorated with a splendid illuminated picture. It showed an old Jew bound in chains, which were being loosened by an angel and laid at the feet of the emperor. Dr. Zevulun and his wife were so impressed by this picture that they were unable to drag themselves away. Suddenly, a strange lady came up and, tapping Dr. Zevulun on the shoulder, whispered something into his ear. He turned as pale as a ghost and could hardly speak.

Fredericka looked at him in surprise as he stammered, "Come away from here. Let us hurry home!"

They returned to their hotel. Dr. Zevulun remained silent, and his young wife lacked the courage to press him for an explanation.

When Fredericka awoke the next morning and looked

at her husband, she was shocked at his appearance. Worried, she asked what was the matter, and he replied that he must have caught a cold the previous night. As he spoke, he pulled out his watch to see the time.

"My watch has stopped," he said. "I must take it to a skillful watchmaker whom I know. I shall be back in a quarter of an hour."

"Have your breakfast before you go!" Fredericka implored him.

"I shall be back by the time breakfast is served. I feel lost without my watch. The watchmaker will lend me another while mine is being repaired."

With these words, he left her.

The young wife got up and dressed, and soon their breakfast was served, for Dr. Zevulun had ordered it before leaving the hotel. Fredericka decided to wait for her husband before eating her own breakfast. However, her coffee grew cold, and her husband had not yet returned. She felt uneasy and paced back and forth impatiently in the room. Ten o'clock, eleven o'clock, at last twelve o'clock passed, and still Dr. Zevulun had not returned. The young wife spent the whole day, a day to which she had been looking forward eagerly, in her room in dreadful anxiety. Evening came, and still Dr. Zevulun had not returned.

Sick with fear and worry, Fredericka lay down on her couch. At last she rang the bell and asked for the manager. He came up and listened to her story in amazement. He advised her to wait till morning and then to inform the police.

What a dreadful night that was for Fredericka! What could have happened to her husband? She listened to the sound of every passing carriage. Several times, carriages stopped in front of the popular hotel. Fredericka would then rush downstairs in order to welcome her returning husband, but each time she found that strangers had arrived. Disappointed, she went back to her room.

It seemed as if the night would never end, but at last it was daybreak. At eight o'clock the manager arrived to take her to the police station. There, the story was heard with great surprise. Dr. Zevulun had not applied for a travel permit. The unhappy woman was asked whether all had been well between her and her husband, whether her husband had much money on him and whether he had left any debts at home. But they had been living together very happily, nothing had disturbed their domestic bliss, not even the unhappy relationship with Fredericka's parents. He did not carry much money with him, at the most, a few gulden. The money set aside for their holiday expenses was safe in their room at the hotel. Their general financial position, too, was excellent. Fredericka's dowry had been well invested in P., and her money had not been touched.

Many days went by. Dr. Zevulun seemed to have disappeared mysteriously without a trace. All police enquiries were fruitless. Had he run away? Why should he have tried to escape such a comfortable and happy life? Could he have been murdered? Why should he have been murdered, since he carried only a few insignificant valuables on him? Could he have met with an accident in broad daylight? Surely some trace of him or his corpse would then have been found? After eight days, Fredericka returned to P. At the station, she hired a carriage and asked to be taken to the house of her parents. They were shocked at their daughter's dreadful appearance, bent with grief. Weeping loudly, Fredericka fell at her father's feet. Mr. Salz raised her up and embraced her.

Her parents were even more shocked when they were told of the mysterious disappearance of their son-in-law. Mr. Salz went to Vienna, accompanied by an experienced detective, but no trace of Dr. Zevulun could be found. Dr. Zevulun had not been seen at any of the numerous watchmakers in the great city.

Mr. Salz was liberal both with his time and his money. He spared neither trouble nor expense in pursuing the search for his son-in-law. Announcements were published in all Austrian and foreign newspapers, offering a reward for the slightest information concerning Dr. Zevulun, but all to no avail—the doctor had disappeared!

III

FORSAKEN

FREDERICKA NOW LIVED WITH her parents again, as before her marriage. The old people tried to soften the hard fate of their daughter by an even greater show of affection. Their earlier disagreements were forgotten, and no word of reproach was ever uttered within hearing of the unfortunate woman. Ten full years passed in this fashion. Then her mother died, and three years later, the father followed her to his grave. Now Fredericka was completely alone in the world.

When the year of mourning for her father had ended, Fredericka, in her loneliness, decided to go on a long journey in order to find some distraction. But the political situation prevented her from traveling in the year 1866. However, in the spring of 1867 she left her hometown in the company of an elderly Christian friend who had offered her services as a lady's companion. They spent only a short time in Vienna, for the beautiful Imperial City brought back too many sad memories. They spent a longer time in Dresden, where the famous portrait gallery especially attracted the attention of the ladies. Once, while they were standing in front of

Murillo's "The Goose Thief," lost in admiration, a gentleman approached them. As it happened, Mr. Laditz too was from P. and a good friend of Fredericka's companion, Mrs. Skopp. He too was on holiday, and his plans were almost identical with those of the ladies. He intended to travel to Berlin, Hamburg and Cologne and from there to the world exhibition in Paris, just as they were planning to. Thus it came about that he was their constant companion.

Mr. Laditz was a handsome man of thirty-six. He had good manners and was well educated in all fields of knowledge. He was a chemist by profession but preferred a literary career. He combined business and pleasure on this journey and made literary contributions as a correspondent for a popular newspaper. He also wrote travel stories for several large newspapers in his hometown. The ladies were greatly amused when he read them reports of the day's events in the evening, or if by chance they found their own local paper in some restaurant and read the report of their travels, in which they themselves were sometimes mentioned, though of course under other names.

Mr. Laditz was extremely considerate and polite to Fredericka, and she soon came to appreciate him as a well-educated man of the world. Mr. Laditz was a Protestant, and it never occurred to Fredericka that his intentions towards her were anything other than merely friendly. Fredericka was now thirty-one years old. Her beauty had ripened with age, and her old grief had long ago healed. She lived happily in the present and never

"No, I am condemned to lead a lonely life. The laws of my religion forbid me to remarry unless the death of my poor husband can be proven," Fredericka replied.

"But isn't a man who has vanished without any trace considered dead after fifteen years?" asked Mrs. Skopp.

"No, never. Definite proof of his death is required. My father often explained that to me."

Mrs. Skopp dropped the subject for the time being, but whenever she was alone with Fredericka, she never missed the opportunity to praise the wonderful qualities of Mr. Laditz. When Mr. Laditz was present, she would turn the conversation to religious problems. The differences between various religions were discussed frequently and at great length. Then Mr. Laditz would declare his great admiration for Jews and Judaism. Of course, as a Christian, he considered Christianity as the superior religion. For him Judaism was a lower degree of Protestantism. He would also point out various Jewish laws which a non-Jew would consider harsh and unduly restrictive.

Then he would add in a conciliatory tone, "But our age, with its humane and progressive ideas, is breaking down these barriers. It is bringing together the extremes and achieving a more balanced view, everywhere uniting all mankind in understanding and tolerance. No matter how many restrictions education has imposed on us, closer personal contacts are producing a situation where men stretch out their hands to one another in brotherhood, leading to a mankind united in its ideals."

He would then continue with a smile, "Besides, it

makes no difference in what form we pay homage to the Sublime Being. A truly educated person will acknowledge the validity of all these forms of worship and never claim heaven as his sole property."

Since Fredericka was completely unable to refute his arguments, such conversations could not fail to leave an impression on her mind. Thus, while at the beginning of the journey she had lived strictly in accordance with Jewish religious laws, gradually she became more lax in her observance. Whenever anything of this nature occurred, Mrs. Skopp would throw a significant look at Mr. Laditz.

Before leaving Berlin they decided to visit several synagogues. It was the Sabbath, and Mr. Laditz had chosen to visit the Orthodox synagogue first. The day was extremely hot, and since the air in the narrow, low and dingy room was suffocating, they left the synagogue before the sermon. "You see," Mr. Laditz said to Fredericka, "that is the Judaism of the past."

From there the friends proceeded to the new, impressive synagogue in the Oranienburgerstrasse. The attractive building made a deep impression on them. The sound of the organ was extremely beautiful, the choir excellent, but the building was empty. The few worshipers appeared lost in the large space, and even these few kept up a continuous whisper among themselves.

"You see," Mr. Laditz told the ladies when he met them at the exit to the ladies' gallery, "that is modern Judaism. It approaches the Protestant form of worship, but a few things are still missing. The seat-holders who pay for those empty seats are still busy in their shops and offices. The modern Jew celebrates Sunday as his holiday just as the Christians do, and like them, he leaves attendance at prayer services to fools and old women. What irony to fix prayer services at a time when everybody is fully occupied with his weekday activities—services which nobody can nor wishes to attend!"

On the following day, Sunday, our friends visited the synagogue of the Reform Jews. The Berlin Reform community, founded in 1846, had moved the weekly day of rest from Saturday to Sunday. In this synagogue, men and women sat together in the same hall, the men with heads bared. Prayers were reduced to a minimum. Hebrew was confined to the *Shemah* and parts of the *Kedushah*. Here, Jewish festivals were always celebrated on Sundays or on Christian holidays. Even on the Day of Atonement worshipers left the synagogue at noon and returned, if convenient, a few hours later. The sermon always avoided specifically Jewish problems, and on the rare occasion when Jewish practices were mentioned, it was only to ridicule them.

"Well," said Fredericka to Mr. Laditz, who had accompanied her, "if you want to be rational, you will call this the Judaism of the future."

"No, my dear," Laditz replied with a smile, "this is not the Judaism of the future, but the religion of the future. It represents a form of pure religion based on reason which has lost almost all trace of its former national and denominational character.

"The Protestants too will develop in this way—we can already see progress in this direction in some modern communities. And so too even the Catholics! Eventually there will be only one church which will honor all great men equally, Jew or Christian, Solon and Lycurgus, Socrates and Plato, Schiller, Goethe, and Garibaldi. Denominational forms of worship will fall away, religious customs and rituals will cease to be observed. Judaism and Christianity will be emancipated from purely external expressions and become united. But a modern educated man and an intelligent woman need not wait for the distant future. They can break these chains now."

Fredericka listened attentively. She became engrossed in her thoughts, and neither Mrs. Skopp nor Mr. Laditz tried to distract her.

IV

ON THE BRINK OF DANGER

THE TOUR WAS ALMOST AT an end. They had seen Hamburg, Cologne and Paris. They had visited the exhibition, where they met various acquaintances and amused themselves. Religious questions had frequently been discussed, and Mr. Laditz found Fredericka a receptive listener. Summer was nearing its end when our friends traveled homewards by steamer on the Rhine. With what pleasure they admired the delightful Rhine valley after the crowds and the turmoil of the noisy capital! One hot, sultry September day, when the air over the water was pleasantly cool, Fredericka and Mrs. Skopp were strolling along the deck. Mr. Laditz joined the ladies and told them the names of the ruined castles which they passed on their journey, recounting delightful and sometimes frightening tales and legends connected with them. The scenery became increasingly attractive and romantic. Slowly the steamer proceeded upstream, but too fast for the traveler who wanted to capture all the delightful sights with his eye. Innumerable ships sailed up and down the green waters.

On both banks of the river were railway lines. The trains seemed to plunge into the mountains, disappear for a few moments and emerge once more on the other side.

"You see," Laditz resumed their conversation when they had gazed silently at the impressive spectacle for a while, "this is a genuine picture of our times. Though the castles of the robber-barons are still stuck on the rocks, they are harmless crumbling ruins now. In contrast, ships wind their way up and down this peaceful river, which is spanned by numerous splendid bridges, while on both its banks trains transport seething crowds of humanity in both directions.

"With the decline of medieval knights and castles and the end of the religious wars of the last centuries, medieval prejudices have also disappeared. All nations and all men have become brothers. At this very moment, a congress which aims at the annihilation of zealots and tyrants and at the establishment of a permanent state of peace for all nations is meeting in Geneva."

Then he remained silent, as if plucking up courage to speak again.

"Fredericka," he continued (he had been calling her by her first name for some time), "we have spent almost four months together. This has been the best time of my life. I have learned to love you. I believe that I am not unworthy of you, Fredericka. Will you marry me?"

Startled, Fredericka cried out, attracting the attention of the other passengers.

"Leave us now," Mrs. Skopp told Laditz. "Let me talk to my friend alone."

Laditz went to the other end of the steamer where he leaned over the rail and gazed at the green waters. Meanwhile, Fredericka sat down and cried bitterly. Mrs. Skopp let her cry for some time. "Well," she said at last, "may our friend cherish any hope?" A fresh stream of tears flowed from Fredericka's eyes.

"Shall I abandon the faith of my fathers, shall I hurt my pious parents in their graves in this way? On no account!" she said.

"But what else will you do? Do you want to spend all your life in mourning? Can you marry again as a Jewess?... Come, let another, more skillful advocate speak for himself."

She called Laditz. "Fredericka," he said after being told by Mrs. Skopp what the poor woman had said, "I would not hesitate for one moment to become a Jew for your sake. Religion to me is only a matter of form. But my friend told me that as a Jewess you will not be permitted to remarry. Therefore I advise you to be baptized and become a Protestant. Then we shall have Dr. Zevulun declared a missing person, and there will be no further obstacle to our marriage."

Fredericka covered her face with both hands and cried, I can't do that! I cannot be baptized!"

"Would you accept my proposal if we could live together as Jews?"

"I admire and value you and could not imagine a better companion in life."

"Well then, I shall make another suggestion. Soon we shall land in a large city which has an old Jewish community and a rabbi who is known even in our hometown. Why not consult this rabbi? If he permits you to marry again, I shall become a Jew. But if you are forbidden to marry, then the only alternative left to you is to exchange the Jewish religion with its rigid laws for the more liberal Protestant faith. Thus you will become a Christian, and a Protestant clergyman will bless our marriage."

Laditz waited silently while Fredericka looked down, deep in thought. Meanwhile, their steamer was approaching the narrows of Bingen. White foam sprayed on deck from the turbulent water.

"Fredericka," Laditz resumed the conversation, "can you see those rocks which break the waves so that they thunder and foam? Those are the 'Binger Narrows.' They used to be much narrower, so that ships passing through here were in mortal danger. Passengers used to fall on their knees and pray, but often their prayers were of no avail. The ship was smashed on the rocks, and people died an untimely death. In modern times people are more intelligent. The rocks have been blasted away, so that ships pass without meeting any obstructions. You too ought to blast away the rocks that obstruct your path so that you can live a free and happy life. Do you agree to my suggestion?"

"I agree," she said, shaking his hand. The three people did not notice the beautiful and historical sites on the shore. They were too engrossed in their own thoughts to be interested in the world outside.

V

A JUST ADVISER

THE RABBI WHOM FREDERIKA wished to consult sat in his study. It was about ten in the morning, and the rabbi had to officiate at a wedding at one o'clock. The Pentateuch lay open in front of him at the weekly protion of *Ki Tavo*. He was looking for a text for his wedding address when he was struck by the following words, "And there shall you build an altar to the Lord your God, an altar of stones; you shall lift up no iron tool upon them. You shall build the altar of the Lord your God of unhewn stones, and shall offer up on it burnt offerings to the Lord your God. And you shall sacrifice peace-offerings and you shall eat there and rejoice before the Lord your God. And you shall write upon the stones all the words of this law very plainly."

The words he had just read appeared to him a suitable text for his wedding sermon. He intended to compare marriage to the altar of God, since, according to our sages, the altar weeps when a man divorces the wife of his youth. The longer the rabbi considered these words of Holy Scripture, the more suitable the text seemed for this occasion. With his mind full of ideas, symbols and points of comparison, he took up his pen to make notes for the sermon.

Then he was informed that a lady wished to speak to him urgently. He gave his consent, and Fredericka was admitted.

"Have I the pleasure of addressing the rabbi?" she asked.

"Yes. I am the rabbi. Will you be seated?"

"Rabbi, I should like your advice on an important matter, or rather, I would appreciate your view on it."

"Please proceed."

"I come from P., and my name is Mrs. Zevulun. My husband was a medical practitioner. A year after our marriage we traveled to Vienna. My husband went out to buy something and never came back. He disappeared without leaving a trace."

"How dreadful! Have you no idea what might have become of your husband?"

"None. We had lived together very happily; our financial position was excellent. He must have met with an accident."

"Has his body been found?"

"No, he has remained lost without a trace. As you can imagine, my father spared no effort to find him—but all was in vain."

"How tragic! You have my sympathy."

"For fifteen years I have mourned for my husband. My parents died during that time, and I am quite alone in the world."

"Your fate is very hard indeed."

"But now I would like to marry again. Am I allowed to do so?"

"You are allowed to marry only if you have clear evidence of your husband's death, or if your husband is still alive and gives you a bill of divorce. Only under these circumstances would you be allowed to marry again."

"Impossible. I am convinced that my husband is no longer alive. Why should he have run away from me? And even if he had deserted me, surely he would have written at least one letter? No, he is no longer alive, but it is quite impossible to prove his death. Since it has been impossible to obtain proof of his death during the last fifteen years, how could we find any evidence now?"

"I pity you and sympathize with you, Mrs. Zevulun, but under the circumstances, you are not permitted to marry again. As long as your husband's death is in doubt, you are still tied to him."

"That is according to Jewish law, sir. But the Protestant church permits remarriage as soon as the missing person has been officially declared dead."

"What are you trying to say?"

"I shall simply have to be baptized in order to be able to marry again."

The rabbi was deeply shocked, but as soon as he had regained his composure, he said, "Madam, as you may know, our holy religion contains six hundred and thirteen commandments. When life is in danger we are allowed to transgress six hundred and ten of them. The patient whose life is in danger may eat on the holiest fast day, and we are allowed to desecrate the Sabbath for his sake. In order to save a life we are permitted to transgress all positive and negative commandments, except for three. These three are so important and so holy that we must sacrifice our lives rather than transgress them. They are murder, adultery and apostasy. You are prepared to commit two of these heinous offences—apostasy and adultery—simultaneously, and you tell me that coolly and calmly!"

"No, no, dear rabbi, not coolly nor calmly. God is my witness! He knows how difficult it is for me to leave the faith of my fathers. But tell me, what else can I do? Shall I mourn in solitude all my life? I am still of an age and in circumstances where I can choose a husband for myself. But I am approaching the end of my youth, and in a few years' time I shall remain alone forever."

"Is it such a terrible misfortune to remain unmarried? Couldn't you choose a career which would distract and entertain you and help you lead a useful life?"

"I have received no training for any career. I have been educated to wealth and learned only social accomplishments. Besides, I have led a sad and lonely life long enough now. I am tired of it. I want to be happy again."

"And do you really think you can acquire so-called happiness by committing two serious crimes?"

"But, Rabbi, you exaggerate! I shall not commit adultery, for I am firmly convinced that my husband is dead. As for the change in religion, surely in our enlightened age we have outgrown those rigid rules. All paths lead to the center, all religions have the same essence and the same aim. Remember, we live in the eighteen hundreds."

"You are mistaken, madam. We may be living in the eighteen hundreds, but no matter how many centuries have passed, the world cannot receive a greater enlightenment than that which was granted to us on Mount Sinai through the light of divine revelation. Adultery, apostasy and murder are the most dreadful crimes. If your parents were still alive, they would have to sit on the ground and mourn for their erring daughter as if she had died."

Fredericka shuddered when she heard this and began to weep bitterly. Then she said with tears in her eyes, "I would like to remain a Jewess, if only you would permit me to marry."

"I cannot give you permission; I am only the mouthpiece and interpreter of the divine law. The Torah forbids remarriage except in one of the two cases which I have already explained to you. Don't imagine that you could ever be happy if you act in defiance of God's law."

"But how could God want that? Why has God put such a heavy burden on me?"

"What man can fathom God's impenetrable and wise plans? Can the crippled, the blind or the dumb ask why God has maimed them? They must bear their lot with resignation. You see, madam, God has allotted you a hard fate. Now you must prove to our Father in Heaven the strength of your character and your sincere love, so that you may learn to bear your fate with resignation and piety. You should say, 'Thou hast decreed it, Lord, Thy holy will be done.' "

"But I lack that sincerity and pious resignation!"

"Then you must try to acquire it."

"I am most grateful to you, dear rabbi. You have told me your views and given me advice. Now I shall make my own decision."

"I pray to the Lord that it may be the right one."

"It will certainly be the right one, at least in my view. Farewell!"

"Good-bye. May the Lord protect you from your passions."

Fredericka left the house; and the rabbi's thoughts followed her sadly for some time. Then he remembered his forthcoming wedding address. With great effort he concentrated on his speech, but his thoughts continually returned to the unhappy, forsaken woman, her hard struggles and her severe temptations. Would she succumb, or would she overcome them? Had his words impressed her? Would he ever hear what she had decided and what had become of her? At last he managed to dismiss all these distressing thoughts and to devote himself again to the duties of his rabbinical position.

VI

THE DECISION

FREDERICKA RETURNED TO the hotel where her friends were staying and found Mr. Laditz and Mrs. Skopp together. They gazed at her expectantly. Fredericka, however, was unable to utter a word. She threw herself into an armchair and cried bitterly.

"Has that hypocrite of a clergyman made things difficult for you?" asked Mr. Laditz.

"I did not meet any hypocritical clergyman," Fredericka replied, regaining her composure. "I met a man who explained to me quietly and firmly the rules of our religion and showed great concern for my cruel fate."

Laditz bit his lip and then asked, "What have you decided to do?"

"I shall go to see a Protestant clergyman, but not here, not here!"

"Then let us travel to F. today."

In F. Fredericka went to see a local Protestant clergyman, who received her kindly. She told him her story and explained clearly the reasons which inclined her to change her religion. At first the clergyman foresaw many difficulties and raised numerous objections. He asked her to return in the afternoon. Meanwhile, Laditz called on him, and when Fredericka came back in the afternoon, the clergyman was more co-operative. He expressed the hope that the truth of Christianity would gradually take root in the mind of the new convert. He was willing to absolve her from a course of religious instruction, since Mr. Laditz, a man versed in Christian tradition, would teach her after their marriage. Thus the baptism could be performed the next day.

Fredericka, who throughout their journey had shared a room with Mrs. Skopp, decided to spend the next night alone to be able to think matters over before taking such a decisive step. Therefore, she asked at the hotel for a single room for herself and had her luggage taken up to it. After the most fervent and sincere prayers, she retired to bed, but for a long time she was unable to sleep.

Her late parents appeared before her eyes repeatedly and looked at her accusingly. At last her eyes closed and she fell asleep, only to start dreaming. Her dream took her to her hometown, to the time when she was still young and had promised Dr. Zevulun to be his forever.

She awoke and was filled with a vague sorrow. She felt that the bond made, in spite of her parents' wishes, was still strong, and yet she wished to tie herself again in a new marriage! She grew restless. Sitting up, she looked at her watch. It was only midnight, and so reluctantly she tossed and turned till she again fell into a restless slumber. She had a terrifying dream. She felt herself tied to two fiery horses. At one side was the rabbi, driving his horse to the east, while on the other side the Protestant clergyman was driving his horse to the west. She was afraid that she would be torn in two and screamed in fear and pain. Then she awoke. What an awakening! Had the dream shown her a picture of her future?

She hid her face in her pillows and fell asleep a third time. This time she dreamed she was back in her parental home. She wanted to greet her parents with a friendly "Good morning," but her father shouted at her, "Go away, you cursed apostate! You are heaping shame on your parents' heads. I wish you had never been born!" Then she fell down at her father's feet, clung to his knees and called out, "Father! I want to remain your daughter. I don't want to be an apostate and be cursed by you. I hope one day to lie next to you in my grave."

Her father rose, embraced and kissed her and called out, "My daughter, we shall meet again in heaven!" Her mother, too, embraced her, shedding tears of joy.

Fredericka awoke a third time, and this time her mind was filled not with pain, sadness and fear but with pure heavenly joy. She got up, lit the candles and dressed herself for a journey. The first train left at five a.m. Quickly, she packed her clothes, wrote a note to Mrs. Skopp and Laditz, rang for the porter, paid her bill and was driven to the station. A few hours later she arrived at the rabbi's house in the city on the Rhine.

"Sir, you helped me by giving me good advice; do not desert me now," she said. Then she told him all that had happened to her since she saw him last.

The rabbi advised her to find accommodation with a respectable Jewish family and to stay in the town for a while, in order to be safe from the attentions of Mr. Laditz and Mrs. Skopp. She followed his advice.

The rabbi wrote to one of his friends in P. and asked him to find out what he could about the characters and personalities of Mr. Laditz and Mrs. Skopp.

A week later his friend wrote back that Mrs. Skopp had brought a court case against Mr. Laditz immediately after their return to P. Mr. Laditz had refused to pay her a promised sum of money, and even her traveling expenses, since the purpose of the journey, i.e., his marriage to the wealthy widow of Dr. Zevulun, had not been accomplished. The rabbi forwarded this letter to the poor deceived woman whose downfall had been so carefully planned.

On reading the letter Fredericka was filled with gratitude and, with tears in her eyes, thanked God for her timely rescue. Then she wrote to the banker in P. with whom her money had been deposited and asked him to pay Mrs. Skopp for the expenses of her journey and to act as an intermediary in order to achieve a peaceful out-of-court settlement at the lowest possible cost. She soon received the reply that Mrs. Skopp was satisfied with the refund of her traveling expenses and was not taking her claims against Mr. Laditz any further.

VII

THE MYSTERY IS UNCOVERED

ONE WEEK BEFORE THE NEW Year, a man who appeared prematurely aged as a result of suffering, entered the study of the rabbi of the above mentioned city on the Rhine.

"Rabbi, I come to ask for your help," he said in a cultured voice. "I have neither papers nor proof of my identity, and the story of my misfortunes will seem as implausible as a fairy tale. I fear you will not believe me."

"Sit down, sir," said the rabbi kindly, "and let me hear your story!"

They both sat down and the stranger began, "My name is Zevulun, and I come from P. where I used to practice as a doctor."

"You are Dr. Zevulun from P.?" the rabbi asked in surprise. The stranger sprang up.

"You have heard of me?" he asked.

"Yes," the rabbi replied. "I know the story of a Dr. Zevulun from P. who disappeared suddenly fifteen years ago."

"Not from P. but from Vienna, where I had gone for a holiday with my young wife," the stranger said.

"And you are truly Dr. Zevulun? For years they have been trying to trace you everywhere, without success. Now you come here and claim to be the man whom the authorities have been looking for in vain. You will excuse me if I say that I cannot possibly accept your story immediately."

"The mystery of my sudden disappearance will be cleared up after I give you a detailed account of my misfortunes."

"Certainly. Please do so!"

"When I was a student in Vienna I led a very dissolute life. My parents were dead and had left me a considerable fortune. As I was young, rich and independent, with no firm religious principles, I soon mixed in disreputable company. Though I studied diligently by day, I always spent my evenings in cheerful company. Through them I met one of the rising stars of the Viennese theater. She was greatly taken by me, the young student. She even abandoned the nobles who were her ardent admirers. I was flattered. She became greatly attached to me, but I grew tired of our relationship after a year and withdrew my attentions. She would not accept this, begging and beseeching for affection, but I remained cold. When she swore to take revenge on me, a terrible, cruel revenge, I laughed at her. Adele left Vienna in order to accept an engagement on the stage of a provincial theater. I, too, on completing my studies and attaining first-class honors, returned to my home town where I soon established a large practice and won a dearly beloved wife. About a year after our wedding, my young wife and I traveled to Vienna, where great celebrations were taking place to honor the emperor's return to Vienna. One evening, when I was walking with my wife in the beautiful illuminated capital, I was suddenly accosted by a lady. Imagine my shock when I recognized Adele! I muttered an excuse and hurried home with my wife. I spent a dreadful night. The revenge threatened so many years earlier by the rejected actress haunted me, and I had a terrible nightmare. I felt as if a snake with the face of Adele was curled around my body and was trying to strangle me."

Dr. Zevulun stopped, exhausted. Even fifteen years later, the memory of his torment greatly upset him.

VIII

ADELE'S REVENGE

IN THE MORNING, I FOUND that my watch had stopped, and I decided to take it for repair immediately," continued Dr. Zevulun. "I had left my hotel and crossed a few streets when a stranger approached me.

" 'Are you Dr. Zevulun from P.?' he enquired urgently.

" 'At your service sir,' I replied.

" 'Please come quickly to see a lady who has been suddenly taken ill. Will you follow me, as there isn't another doctor in the vicinity?' I followed him, not suspecting a trap, and he led me to a beautiful house. In an elegant drawing room on a sofa sat Adele. I was frightened as soon as I saw her and looked around for my guide, but he had disappeared.

" 'Where is the patient?' I asked.

" 'Here,' said Adele. 'I am the patient. You remember me, Zevulun, don't you?'

" 'I remember you, Miss. But since you appear to be perfectly well, I see no cause to remain.'

" 'Zevulun, why should you rush away from a friend whom you haven't seen for so many years? Sit down next to me for a while; I have so much to tell you!'

"Adele then told me that she had become very wealthy. Her brother happened to be in California where deposits of gold were discovered. He had amassed an enormous fortune and later returned to Europe with his wealth. But his health had been undermined abroad, and he soon died, leaving his fortune to her, his only sister.

"Adele implored me to return to her, to share her wealth and live a life of pleasure and abundance in a distant country. She offered me all her treasures unconditionally, but I remained firm in spite of all her blandishments. I refused to give up my young wife and my comfortable, honorable position in P. I was determined to win the respect of my parents-in-law and quite unwilling to go back to sin and vice. When Adele realized that all her demands and pleas were useless, she jumped up in fury. 'Then you shall suffer my revenge, you faithless creature!' she exclaimed, and rang a bell.

"Two men rushed in and trussed me up. The liquid which they forced me to swallow made me lose consciousness. When I awoke I was wearing a straitjacket like a lunatic and was sitting in a railway compartment. The two men who had tied me up were sitting opposite me. I didn't know them but discovered recently that they carried a passport which permitted them to take a lunatic to a famous London asylum.

"I don't wish to trouble you with a description of that nightmarish journey. All went well for my guards. We arrived in London where I was taken to a private nursing home for mental patients. That furious woman must have paid them an immense sum of money to keep me there.

"At first I was rebellious and wanted to force them to release me, but the most ruthless forms of punishment soon calmed me. My fate was so cruel that I feared I would really lose my reason. Then a small Hebrew prayer book which I had carried about with me for my wife's use, and which they had left with me, came to my rescue. I prayed daily and gained serenity and peace of mind as well as the courage to bear my awful fate. Now I bore my lot with resignation and thus was allowed greater freedom in the nursing home. Being a doctor, I was able to use the opportunity to make a more detailed study of mental diseases, which I could often observe at close quarters. Nurses, doctors and patients soon came to like me, but I dared not mention the fact that I was healthy and imprisoned there unlawfully. That would have cost me my precious bit of freedom, at least temporarily, and exposed me to the dangers of further maltreatment.

"In this way, I spent fourteen years. Last year a new inmate entered the institution, and as a result of my apparent docility, I was unexpectedly allowed to be alone with him. I soon realized that he too was healthy. He had been sent there by his greedy relations who wished to inherit his fortune. They had called in unscrupulous doctors to certify him as mad. We soon came to understand each other. By a combined effort and the promise of a huge reward, we managed to persuade one of the warders to pass a letter on to the solicitors of Sir Oliver, as my fellow sufferer was called. The letter was effective. Suddenly a royal commission consisting of court doctors appeared in the nursing home and demanded to see Sir Oliver. The director, however, had prepared for this eventuality. Sir Oliver received a heavy blow on the back of his head which knocked him almost unconscious, so that to the commission he appeared insane. These doctors were thus satisfied and about to leave the home when I managed to approach them and inform them how Sir Oliver had come by his apparent insanity. They turned back and waited. Gradually, the unconscious man came round and revealed to the doctors the entire intrigue of which he had been the victim. I also spoke up and told them of my sad fate. I managed to convince the commission that I was entirely normal like any other healthy man. Thus, both Sir Oliver and I were set free immediately, and the director of the asylum was arrested. The case against him is still in progress, and he will probably be deported to a criminal settlement.

"Rabbi, can you imagine the wonderful joy of freedom regained? I was like a man arisen from the dead. The thought of what had become of my wife obsessed me, and Sir Oliver gave me the necessary sum of money to travel home.

"But the long stay in that awful prison had made me careless. On the way, in Calais, my suitcase containing my wallet was stolen from me. I could have stayed there and written to London asking Sir Oliver for more money, or written to P. But then I would have had to wait in Calais for a few days, and I was desperate to reach home. I preferred to sell my watch and my ring hoping that the money these brought me would pay my fares home to P. Unfortunately, I was wrong. My state of health only allowed me to travel slowly. Therefore, I had to stop overnight in various places, and my money lasted only as far as this town. Could you arrange for me to receive fifty gulden as a loan, Rabbi? Perhaps a wealthy fellow Jew would be willing to do me this kind service?"

"My dear sir," replied the rabbi, "your story bears the stamp of truth. I have listened to it with more interest than you would suspect. But how can you prove your identity?"

"That is impossible for me here, though there are hundreds of people in P. who would recognize me."

The rabbi was in a quandary. What could he do? Should he tell the stranger that his wife was here in the same town? But who could confirm the truth of his story? It appeared to be true, but he had not yet given any proof of his identity. The rabbi recalled several instances of deceitful individuals who had attempted to acquire rich, deserted wives. They had told elaborate lies, appearing to be true, to try to prove that they were the long lost husband. Fredericka herself would be deceived even more easily than a disinterested stranger.

Suddenly, the rabbi recalled that two respectable Orthodox Jewish merchants from P. were staying in the nearby health resort of W. They had paid him a visit a few weeks ago and told him that they intended to stay in

W. until after the New Year. Perhaps they would be able to identify the stranger.

"Sir," he addressed him at last, "in the nearby spa of W. are two of your fellow citizens whose names I have forgotten. But I remember the name of their hotel and thus can easily find them. May I take you to them? They will surely advance you the required sum of money."

The stranger agreed and thus they took the next train to W

IX

REUNION

THE MERCHANTS FROM P., Mr. Weisenbom and Mr. Winerstein, were about to leave the Four Seasons Hotel for a walk on the promeade, when a carriage stopped outside the hotel. Mr. Winerstein recognized one of the occupants, the rabbi, immediately.

"Hello, Rabbi!" he called cheerfully. "Were you coming to pay us a visit?"

Wiesenbom, however, stared in stupefaction at the rabbi's companion. "Surely that is Dr. Zevulun or his double!" he exclaimed. "Zevulun, Zevulun, is it really you?"

"Winerstein and Weisenbom, my old friends, are you real or am I dreaming?" Zevulun called out and alighted to embrace his friends. The two merchants invited the rabbi and Zevulun to their room in the hotel. First Zevulun had to tell his story. He recounted briefly the history of his misfortune which is already familiar to us. Then the two merchants related all they knew about Fredericka and her deceased parents.

So far, the rabbi had listened quietly, but now he spoke.

"Now my turn has come to tell you something. I am also involved in this affair!" he said.

The others listened attentively as he told them about the latest developments: of Fredericka's travels and the temptations she had overcome and the revelation of the contemptible intrigue of which she had been the intended victim. When at last the rabbi concluded, Dr. Zevulun enquired, "And where is my poor wife now?"

"In my home town," the rabbi replied.

"Take me to her quickly, quickly," exclaimed Zevulun.

"Not so fast, my dear sir. I must first prepare the poor lady for this pleasant shock. Let us all travel back to my house together, where you and your friends can wait in my study. I shall ask her to call on me immediately and talk to her in the waiting room. Then we shall see what is to be done."

This is exactly what they did.

When Fredericka was shown into his lounge, the rabbi said to her, "I have asked you to come here in order to tell you something most important. I have had news concerning your lost husband."

"Surely, he is not still alive?"

"He is alive."

"Has he deliberately deserted me?"

"No, he has not. Did you ever hear of an actress called Adele?"

"Indeed, I did. My late father told me that Zevulun had been involved with a woman of that name during his years of study. Could he have left me for her sake?"

"No, no, not at all, Madam, do not upset yourself. I shall tell you the full story."

Then the rabbi told her. Tears of anguish flowed from the eyes of the unfortunate woman when she heard of the tortures her husband had suffered. Her love for her husband was reawakened with all its old fervor.

"Where is he now?" she exclaimed, when the rabbi had concluded his recital. "He should come to me at once. I want to be his wife again, his faithful and devoted wife!"

Then the rabbi left to call her husband. Nobody was present at their reunion, but from the next room they could hear the two voices, weeping in unison.

X

THE END

After the feast of tabernacles, the rabbi received the following letter:

P. 29th October, 1867

Dear Rabbi,

You will have received my letter with renewed expressions of our gratitude on the eve of the New Year. I am writing now to tell you about the lives of the people to whose happiness you have contributed so much.

We have settled down here again, and I have regained my large practice. As you can imagine, our unusual story has aroused much interest, and we have become star attractions in our social circle. Many patients only come to me in order to talk to me personally, or even to catch a glimpse of me.

We conduct our home in traditional Jewish fashion, and both my wife and I are firmly resolved not to deviate in the slightest from God's commandments. In times of grief and misery one learns to look upward to our Father in Heaven and to pray to Him alone for temporary and eternal bliss.

I have been informed from London that the director of the mental home and his confederates have been condemned to long years of deportation. I have been awarded a considerable sum of money in compensation.

Adele has withdrawn from the punitive arm of justice, at least on this earth. She has lost her reason and is now confined to a mental home. As our sages teach us, "measure for measure."

Mr. Laditz has escaped to America, leaving heavy debts unpaid. I gather that a case of fraud is being brought against him.

Mrs. Skopp hardly dares leave her home. She has become loathsome to all who know her.

Please accept again our most sincere expressions of gratitude. I hardly dare to think what would have become of us without you. Supposing my wife had turned to a Reform rabbi who would have told her that even in matrimonial affairs the law of the land takes precedence over Jewish law? There have been several cases in Berlin and Hamburg recently where deserted wives have remarried without previous Jewish divorce. Thus, Laditz might have become a Jew and my wife... Still, I had better not speak about that. The very thought of it makes me feel ill.

As for you, dear rabbi, may the Lord bless you always. May He give you strength and resolution in your holy task and fulfill all the wishes of your noble heart.

Now we would like you to do us one more favor.

Please publish our story so that it may serve as a warning to others in a similar position. Please change the names of the people involved and disguise the name of our town. Although many people are likely to guess our identity, since our story has become widely known, that does not matter.

You have already shown us so much love and kindness that we feel confident you will not refuse us this last request.

In deep admiration, I remain,

Yours sincerely,

Dr. Zevulun